The image of a ... Raine's retinas

Leaf shaded and dark, its stillness failed to draw her. It repelled instead. Frightening. Repugnant.

Then the surface of the water began to stir. The pond took on a reddish hue. Cold and dark. Bloody and violent.

Unconsciously she opened her mouth, attempting to draw air into lungs that felt as if the pressure of those black depths were closing in on her. The surface continued to churn, patterns emerging as the water roiled.

There were images there, too, but they were moving too quickly for her to focus on any one of them. Like the bits of glass in a kaleidoscope, they merged and blended, changing even as she watched.

She began to fight. To struggle against the pull of the vortex at the center of the pond, trying not to look into its dark heart, because she knew that if she did, she would see something she didn't want to see. Something no one was intended to see.

Dear Harlequin Intrigue Reader,

Temperatures are rising this month at Harlequin Intrigue! So whether our mesmerizing men of action are steaming up their love lives or packing heat in high-stakes situations, July's lineup is guaranteed to sizzle!

Back by popular demand is the newest branch of our Confidential series. Meet the heroes of NEW ORLEANS CONFIDENTIAL—tough undercover operatives who will stop at nothing to rid the streets of a crime ring tied to the most dangerous movers and shakers in town. *USA TODAY* bestselling author Rebecca York launches the series with *Undercover Encounter*—a darkly sensual tale about a secret agent who uses every resource at his disposal to get his former flame out alive when she goes deep undercover in the sultry French Quarter.

The highly acclaimed Gayle Wilson returns to the lineup with *Sight Unseen*. In book three of PHOENIX BROTHERHOOD, it's a race against time to prevent a powerful terrorist organization from unleashing unspeakable harm. Prepare to become entangled in *Velvet Ropes* by Patricia Rosemoor—book three in CLUB UNDERCOVER—when a clandestine investigation plunges a couple into danger….

Our sassy inline continuity SHOTGUN SALLYS ends with a bang! You won't want to miss *Lawful Engagement* by Linda O. Johnston. In Cassie Miles's newest Harlequin Intrigue title—*Protecting the Innocent*—a widow trapped in a labyrinth of evil brings out the Achilles' heel in a duplicitous man of mystery.

Delores Fossen's newest thriller is not to be missed. *Veiled Intentions* arouses searing desires when two bickering cops pose as doting fiancés in their pursuit of a deranged sniper!

Enjoy our explosive lineup this month!

Denise O'Sullivan
Senior Editor, Harlequin Intrigue

SIGHT UNSEEN
GAYLE WILSON

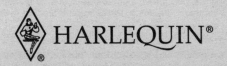

TORONTO • NEW YORK • LONDON
AMSTERDAM • PARIS • SYDNEY • HAMBURG
STOCKHOLM • ATHENS • TOKYO • MILAN • MADRID
PRAGUE • WARSAW • BUDAPEST • AUCKLAND

ISBN 0-373-22784-1

SIGHT UNSEEN

Copyright © 2004 by Mona Gay Thomas

This edition published by arrangement with Harlequin Books S.A.

® and TM are trademarks of the publisher. Trademarks indicated with ® are registered in the United States Patent and Trademark Office, the Canadian Trade Marks Office and in other countries.

www.eHarlequin.com

Printed in U.S.A.

ABOUT THE AUTHOR

Five-time RITA® Award finalist and RITA® Award winner Gayle Wilson has written over thirty novels and three novellas for Harlequin/Silhouette. She has won more than forty awards and nominations for her work.

Gayle still lives in Alabama, where she was born, with her husband of thirty-four years. She loves to hear from readers. Write to her at P.O. Box 3277, Hueytown, AL 35023. Visit Gayle online at www.booksbygaylewilson.com.

Books by Gayle Wilson

HARLEQUIN INTRIGUE
344—ECHOES IN THE DARK
376—ONLY A WHISPER
414—THE REDEMPTION OF DEKE SUMMERS
442—HEART OF THE NIGHT
461—RANSOM MY HEART*
466—WHISPER MY LOVE*
469—REMEMBER MY TOUCH*
490—NEVER LET HER GO
509—THE BRIDE'S PROTECTOR**
513—THE STRANGER SHE KNEW**
517—HER BABY, HIS SECRET**
541—EACH PRECIOUS HOUR
561—HER PRIVATE BODYGUARD†
578—RENEGADE HEART†
591—MIDNIGHT REMEMBERED†
637—NIGHT AND DAY
        "Day"
685—RAFE SINCLAIR'S REVENGE‡
721—ROCKY MOUNTAIN MAVERICK
743—UNDER SURVEILLANCE‡
784—SIGHT UNSEEN‡

*Home to Texas
**Men of Mystery
†More Men of Mystery
‡Phoenix Brotherhood

CIA AGENT PROFILE

Name: Ethan Snow

Date of Birth: January 15, 1968

Assigned Team: External Security

Special Skills: ATP-rated pilot; speaks Russian and Farsi; expert marksman; degree in forensic accounting

Agent Evaluation: Highly disciplined; exhibits stellar leadership qualities; has high expectations of those who work with him

Status: Resigned from the agency due to personal reasons

Current Address: The Phoenix Brotherhood

CAST OF CHARACTERS

Ethan Snow—Phoenix operative Ethan Snow has spent the past six months trying to connect the dots that would tie The Covenant to terrorism. Despite his frustration, he would never willingly have consulted clairvoyant Raine McAllister, no matter how highly recommended she came. He is left no choice, however, when someone in that secret organization makes Raine a target.

Raine McAllister—Had worked on the CIA's remote viewing projects when she was a child. Now she helps the police locate abducted children. When she's asked to help make the connection between those long-ago projects and The Covenant, she discovers that she has more at stake in this investigation than anyone else.

Griff Cabot—The head of the Phoenix will do anything to protect his family, and they are all involved in the danger this time.

Montgomery Gardner—The former DCI oversaw the Agency's experiments in the paranormal. What part of the blame does he bear for Project Cassandra, the one that went terribly wrong?

Sabina Marguery—Her husband's suicide resulted from the failure of Cassandra. What secrets is she harboring about that long-ago experiment? And more important, what secrets is she harboring about Raine McAllister?

Carl Steiner—Is the assistant deputy director of the CIA stonewalling the Phoenix about Cassandra because even after a quarter of a century, the Agency still has something to hide?

Charles Ellington—He wrote the book on the CIA's involvement in parapsychology. Why is Cassandra his only omission?

For Maddie, the sunshine of my life

Prologue

Washington, D.C.

"I've heard of The Covenant, of course. Most of what I know concerns the quasi-patriotic/religious programs they sponsor from behind the scenes. Anyone who's been in Washington for any length of time has some knowledge of their role in those. That's *not* to say, however, that I have anything to add to what you've uncovered. Or any names to give you. No acquaintance of mine has ever admitted to belonging."

Despite his age, former director of central intelligence Montgomery Gardner's mind was still sharp and his connections as good as they had ever been. If he knew nothing about The Covenant, then Phoenix operative Ethan Snow knew he was at a dead end. And that he'd just spent six months on an investigation that was literally going nowhere.

If the stakes hadn't been so high, he might have given up long before now. He had come to Griff Cabot's office today ready to admit defeat. Although Griff had acknowledged that visiting the old man was a last-ditch effort, he had insisted it was one they should make. Gardner was, after all, his wife's grandfather and Griff trusted him to tell them the truth. Now this, too, appeared as futile as every other avenue of information Ethan had pursued.

"What we've *uncovered* is little more than the fact the organization exists," Griff admitted. "And that some of its members, maybe a fringe element, have been involved in funding domestic terrorism."

"Other than a few tantalizing hints," Ethan added, "we can't even get a handle on how wide scale their efforts there have been."

He had hoped the plot involving the Lockett Legacy that John Edmonds had quashed might be an aberration. Now, after months of following up every elusive lead through electronic intercepts and banking records, Ethan had come to believe The Covenant was indeed promoting terrorism on many other fronts. All of them harmful to the United States.

He couldn't prove what he knew intuitively. And he couldn't find any way to penetrate the veil of secrecy that effectively protected whoever was behind the organization.

"Americans perpetrating acts of terror against their own people," Gardner said, shaking his head.

As the director of the CIA, Gardner had certainly been exposed to the harsh realities of treason. There was not a naive bone in the old man's body, yet he sounded shocked that a group considered by many to be both patriotic and altruistic might be guilty of that heinous crime.

"And protected by an oath of confidentiality while they do it," Cabot added.

"Membership is by invitation only," Ethan said. "No one I've interviewed will admit to knowing anyone who is or who might be a member. There are no organizational lists as far as we can discover. No tax records because of the way they handle contributions. I'm not sure any one member is allowed to know the identity of another."

"That must make for interesting meetings," the old man said dryly. "Do you suppose they go to those masked? A modern-day Hell Fire Club?"

"One bent on destruction rather than debauchery," Ethan said.

"And all the while hidden behind a cloak of sanctity," Griff added. "Short of divine intervention or clairvoyance, I'm not sure how we pierce that veil of secrecy."

"I can't help you there," Monty Gardner said, "although I suspect my relationship to the Divinity is as close as some others' in this town who go out of their way to flaunt their standing with Him."

They waited as the old man's lips pursed, his eyes focused unseeingly across the room. The silence stretched long enough to become uncomfortable before Griff broke it.

"Monty?"

"I may know someone who *can* help. You'll have to do a bit of traveling. I assume you aren't averse to that?"

The question was clearly addressed to Ethan. Despite his failure to make any headway with the investigation, this was still his case. If the ex-DCI had a contact he believed could provide information on The Covenant, Ethan was eager to pursue it, wherever it might take him.

"I'm more than willing, if you think it might help."

"I shall hold you to that," the old man said with that same touch of dry humor. "Come into my office, and I'll find the address for you. I keep it in a special place. A *very* special place."

With that cryptic comment, the old man began to rise from his comfortable armchair. Under the cover of that movement, Ethan glanced toward Griff, his brows raised in inquiry.

Cabot shook his head and shrugged. Apparently he had

no idea where or to whom Gardner intended to send his agent.

And it didn't really matter, Ethan acknowledged. Wherever it was, after six months of frustration, he was more than ready to contact anyone who might be able to help.

Chapter One

Two Days Later
Gulf Shores, Alabama

The same vague feeling of discontent that had plagued her throughout the day had driven Raine McAllister to the studio at the back of the beach house at sundown. Usually, simply entering that room, with its wide expanses of glass, instilled a sense of peace. Tonight even its magic didn't seem to be working.

She walked over to the wall of windows that looked out on the blue-green waters of the Gulf of Mexico. Cream-crested waves foamed over the sugar-sand beach below. The red of the dying sun painted the edge of the horizon, but twilight had already fallen over the shoreline.

There was not another human being as far as the eye could see. Living this far from the so-called civilization of the tourist areas had its disadvantages, but the isolation soothed her soul.

Except tonight. Tonight nothing seemed soothing. Or normal. It was as if she viewed the familiar scene below through a lens that was slightly out of focus. Flawed and distorted.

She leaned her forehead against the coolness of the glass

and closed her eyes. She concentrated on breathing deeply, willing her mind to tranquility.

After a moment, far sooner than she had intended, her eyes opened. She listened, but whatever had disturbed her reverie apparently hadn't been sound. There was no noise but the rhythmic sibilance of the waves, muted by the glass.

Whatever was out of place in her world wasn't outside. It was within. Inside her mind. Or in her soul, perhaps. And she had no explanation for it.

She moved away from the window as the sun dipped beyond the ocean, instantly changing the quality of light in the studio. A silver arrow on the water pointed to the moon, which, hidden until now, rode low in the sky.

She lifted the cloth off her latest work and then stepped back to examine the sculpture in its entirety. Like everything else around her, the figure of the running man seemed slightly wrong, but she couldn't pinpoint exactly what it was about the shape that bothered her.

When she'd finished work last night, she had been pleased with her progress. Now, however…

She allowed her eyes to examine each element of her creation. The runner's torso expressed a more solid strength than the long, muscled legs, extended to their full range of motion. She reached out, intending to run her finger down the delicate delineation of the calf muscle she had been so proud of yesterday.

For some reason her hand hesitated in midair, as if reluctant to make contact. Determined to shake off tonight's malaise by losing herself in her work—as she always could—she forced her fingers forward until their sensitive tips encountered the coolness of the clay.

As soon as they did, the figure of the runner disappeared, flickering out of sight to be replaced by the image of a pond. Leaf-shaded and dark, its stillness failed to draw her, as anything in nature normally would. It repelled instead. Frightening. Repugnant.

Deliberately, she jerked her mind away from it, blinking to destroy a picture for which she had no explanation. Her breath trembled in and out in small, audible gasps. Her fingers again hovered a centimeter away from the out-stretched leg of the statue.

She closed her eyes, once more attempting to control her breathing. Attempting to remember the last time something like this had happened.

And when she did, she also remembered why she had vowed that would be the last time. There had been a reason then, of course, but as for whatever she had seen tonight...

She opened her eyes, forcing them to focus on the lines of the statue her hands had molded. Yesterday she had rel-ished the feel of the clay beneath her fingers. The medium had become, as it sometimes did, a living force, responding to her command, but also drawing her where it wanted her to go.

Never before, however, had anything like this happened when she touched it. This, then, was the cause of the fore-boding she'd felt all day. She had known something in her world had changed, but not what. Of all the possible sce-narios she might have imagined to explain her unease, this would have been the last.

That was over. She had sworn it. No more.

She dropped the hand that had touched the statue, turning to retrieve the dampened cloth to place it back over the figure of the runner. Holding the fabric in both hands, she began to drop it onto the half-finished piece.

This time the image exploded on her retinas, the flash as powerful as lightning. The same pond. The same instanta-neous awareness of its inherent evil.

As she watched, unable to break free from the grip of

the vision, the surface of the water began to stir. Gradually, so gradually that it took her several seconds to realize what was happening, the pond took on a reddish hue.

Not the warm, vibrant color of the sunset she had watched over the ocean, but something cold and dark. Bloody and violent.

Unconsciously she opened her mouth, attempting to draw air into lungs that felt flat, as if the pressure of those black depths were closing in on her. The surface continued to churn, patterns emerging as the water roiled.

There were images there, too, she realized, but they were moving too quickly for her to focus on any one of them. Like the bits of glass in a kaleidoscope, they merged and blended, changing even as she watched.

Everything else faded away. The night sky and the ocean. Her work, scattered on tables and pedestals around the studio. Any sense of time. Of self.

She had no idea how long it was before she realized that the patterns were repeating. Echoing one another in slightly differing versions. And that each time they did, they became more vivid. Clearer. More threatening.

She began to fight them. To struggle against the pull of the vortex at the center of the pond around which everything seemed to revolve, trying not to look into its dark heart because she knew that if she did, she would see something she didn't want to see. Something no one was intended to see.

She would never know if she might have won that battle. Just as she had begun to despair of freeing herself from the vision, the old-fashioned chimes on her front door sounded. Rich and melodic, the notes cut through the growing sense of horror that held her captive.

She blinked, and the image disappeared to be replaced by the unfinished sculpture of the runner. The damp cloth she had held in her hands had been carefully draped over it, the folds smoothed around its shape.

She couldn't remember doing that. She couldn't remember anything after she had allowed the center of the cloth to touch the head of the figure.

She glanced toward the windows, surprised to find that the moon was high in the sky, the trail it left across the water now narrow and indistinct. And there was no longer any hint of crimson along the edge of the ocean.

She turned back to the runner, shrouded now by the cloth. Slowly her head moved from side to side in denial of what had just occurred.

The bell chimed again, echoing in the stillness. She wasn't expecting a visitor. She got the occasional solicitor out here, but they never came at night.

"Coming," she said, although there was no way anyone at the front door could hear her from back here. Certainly not that slightly tremulous whisper.

She turned, hurrying now that she had decided something must be wrong. Perhaps the vision had been a warning. A premonition of the news whoever was ringing her doorbell would bring.

Even the suggestion that there might be a logical explanation for what had just happened made her feel better. Never before had anything like that occurred without her consciously seeking it. Her "gift" had always been hers to control. Hers to use or not.

She couldn't imagine living her life any other way. She didn't want to think about having to.

"MAY I HELP YOU?"

Although Gardner hadn't offered to show Ethan any photographs of the woman he'd sent him to see, there had been two small snapshots attached to the inside front cover of the file the old man had taken from his desk. Ethan had studied them, inconveniently upside down, while Gardner copied down Raine McAllister's address.

One of the pictures had been of a freckle-nosed child, smiling broadly at the camera. The other had been of a seemingly self-possessed young woman in a cap and gown, obviously taken at her graduation from college.

The sea-green eyes of the woman holding the door were exactly the same as they had been in the photos—clear and very direct. Her hair was dark, almost black, but the strong sun of the area where she lived had gilded highlights along its entire length. She wore it shoulder length, as straight as she had during her years in college.

Her face, becomingly tanned, was devoid of makeup. The freckles, although fainter, were still visible across the bridge of a rather high-arched, patrician nose.

"My name is Ethan Snow," he said, watching the small furrow form between her brows as she realized it meant nothing to her. "We have a mutual friend who thought you might be willing to be of some assistance—"

The furrow disappeared as her mouth tightened. "Whoever sent you was mistaken. I don't do that anymore."

She stepped back. Her hand, which had never released the knob, began to push the door forward.

Six months of frustration as well as the events of the last forty-eight hours fueled Ethan's anger. He'd be damned if he'd come all this way and not even get an opportunity to tell her why. He put his left forearm against the door, his fingers wrapping around the edge to keep it from moving.

Shocked, she looked up, straight into his eyes. Her pupils had dilated, expanding rapidly into the rim of color. "What the hell do you think you're doing?"

"All you have to do is listen," he said, still holding the door. "If you want to say no after that, fine. But not until."

"You've been misinformed." Her voice was softer, free of the shock and indignation he'd just heard in her question. It sounded more regretful than angry. Or resigned. At least when she added, "I really can't help you."

"You don't even know what I want."

"It doesn't matter. Whatever it is, I can't do it."

Again she pushed against the door, attempting to close it. Ethan didn't remove his arm. Nor did he step back.

"Ten minutes," he said.

He was tired. He was hungry. And given the events of the last two days, there was no way in hell he was going to get in the jet and head back to D.C. without at least finding out why Monty Gardner had given him this woman's name.

Raine McAllister didn't look like any intelligence operative he'd ever met. And she certainly didn't look like a Beltway insider. Not in those skin-tight cutoffs and a tank top.

Even before he and Griff had talked to the old man, however, Ethan had reached the end of his resources. Now, after what had happened last night, he was even more convinced than he had been then that The Covenant was too dangerous to allow him to give up on this investigation.

"Whatever you're here for," Raine McAllister said, "whoever sent you, I really *can't* help you."

She had stopped pushing against the door with her slender strength. She simply stood there, her eyes holding his, her face as empty of expression as her voice had been of emotion.

"Montgomery Gardner."

Before he had completed the enunciation of the last name, her face changed. Then, exactly as the old man's had two nights ago, her eyes seemed to focus on something other than the present. After perhaps five seconds, she closed her mouth, pressing her lips together before she stepped back, opening the door wide enough for Ethan to step through.

Chapter Two

"Exactly what does Mr. Gardner think I can do for you?"

After directing him to the couch, Raine McAllister had perched on an ottoman that belonged to one of the two tall fan chairs in the sunroom she'd led him to. Although there was no ocean view from here, the atmosphere created by white wicker furniture, with its pale-green and yellow cushions, left no doubt this was a beach house.

The room was both elegant and comfortable. During the day, it would be full of light from the floor-to-ceiling windows. Tonight their jalousies had been closed against the darkness, but with the woodwork painted white and the walls a nearly colorless shell pink, the effect was still spacious and airy.

"I'm trying to gather information about The Covenant."

There was a heartbeat of silence. Ethan wasn't sure if that was because she didn't recognize the name or because she was reluctant to reveal to a stranger that she knew anything about the organization.

Given the cloak of secrecy that shrouded The Covenant's operations and considering how dangerous he believed the group to be, either was a possibility. He was hopeful, of course, that the latter of the two explanations was the one that made her hesitate.

"*That's* why he sent you? To find out if I can provide you with information about… I'm sorry. What was it? A covenant?"

Despite what the old man had implied, Raine McAllister seemed genuinely puzzled by the reference. The sinking feeling in the pit of Ethan's stomach reflected his disappointment.

"*The* Covenant," Ethan corrected. "He gave me your name and address and indicated you might be able to help with an ongoing investigation that otherwise, quite frankly, seems to have reached a dead end."

"So…Mr. Gardner sent you here for my help, but he didn't tell you how or why I might be able to give it? And you didn't ask."

He couldn't quite read her tone. Bemused, perhaps? Or maybe *amused,* he amended. Because he'd come all the way down here from Washington based only on an old man's recommendation that she *might* be able to help him?

At the same time he was aware that he'd been let in only because he'd invoked the name of Montgomery Gardner. He didn't want to destroy whatever advantage that had given him by saying something that could be construed as derogatory about the old man. Not before he was sure this really was the wild-goose chase he was beginning to believe it might be.

"Since Mr. Gardner is both a former DCI and a lifelong resident of the D.C. area, when he suggested I talk to you, I assumed you had either worked at the agency or had some specialized knowledge that he believed might be useful."

There was a moment's hesitation, as she appeared to think about what he'd just said.

"I suppose in a way I *did* work for him. I guess I just never looked at it like that."

"You didn't consider what you did at the agency work?"

Even as he posed the question, he was trying to figure out how this woman could have worked for Monty Gardner, whose tenure at the CIA had ended almost twenty-five years ago. He would have guessed her to be in her late twenties. Early thirties at the outside. In either case, she would have been far too young to have been an operative during the old man's regime.

"As far as I was concerned, we played games."

"Games?"

"They'd point to some place on a map, and I'd describe to them what was there."

Suddenly everything he hadn't understood when she'd opened the door clicked into place. And he felt like a fool that he hadn't put it together sooner.

Short of divine intervention or clairvoyance, Griff had said, *I'm not sure how we pierce that veil of secrecy.* And in response, the old man had denied any special pull with the Divinity and had suggested they contact this woman.

Both he and Griff had missed the significance of the thing Gardner *hadn't* denied knowledge of. *Clairvoyance.* Raine McAllister was a clairvoyant.

Ethan knew very little about the CIA's experimentation with parapsychology—other than the fact that it had occurred in response to the Soviet Union's psychic research. And the time frame in which it had taken place fit into the era when Gardner had been the head of the agency, he realized.

It even made sense of the picture in the old man's file. It was obvious Raine had been a little girl when she'd taken part in those experiments.

There was something about the exploitation of a child, despite the genuine concerns about national security during those years, that troubled him. It must have bothered Gardner, as well. Why else would he have kept in touch with this woman all this time?

"You were part of the CIA's psychic research program."

He had thought the old man must be onto something, especially in view of what had happened after his and Griff's visit. Now it seemed that must have occurred, not because Gardner had any information to share, but simply because they'd asked him if he did.

"Something which, judging from your tone, has apparently fallen out of favor," she suggested.

"A long time ago," he said. "Probably because it didn't prove to be as valuable as they'd hoped. I never realized the project involved children."

His discomfort with that scenario undoubtedly showed. She smiled as if amused at his naiveté.

"I take it Mr. Gardner also failed to mention what I was doing *before* they brought me to Langley."

There was an almost challenging tilt to Raine's chin. Ethan wasn't sure where she was headed with the question, but since Gardner had given him no clue about her, either before or after she'd been involved with the CIA, he told her the truth.

"He said nothing about you beyond his hope that you could help with the matter I mentioned. Information about The Covenant."

"Maybe he was trying to spare me embarrassment."

"Embarrassment?" *Where the hell was this going?*

"I told fortunes. Read palms and auras. I even read the cards."

"Tarot?"

Despite the polite tone of his question, Ethan was furious at how much time he'd wasted coming down here. What she was saying now was only what he'd expected when he had finally realized her connection with the agency. Carnival sideshow quackery.

"Occasionally I'd see something about the person I was reading that was…tragic. The first beating I ever got was for telling someone they were going to die," she said with a laugh. "I didn't know any better. I didn't understand the concept of entertaining the customer."

The word *beating* had tightened the muscles in his stomach, although it had been uttered without any inflection. Maybe she'd used the term in jest. An exaggeration of the spankings that were fairly typical methods of discipline when they'd both been children. Something in her eyes belied that comforting thought.

"So you see, I *liked* playing Mr. Gardner's little games," she said. "They were undemanding. And they were safe."

"Then perhaps you'd be willing to play another."

Despite his anger and skepticism, Ethan found he was holding his breath as he waited for her answer. He must be even more desperate than he'd thought.

"For you?"

"For your country."

Her mouth was a little wide in proportion to the rest of her features. The corners ticked up quickly before she looked down at her hands, intertwined in her lap. Slim and tanned, they seemed as delicate as her face. When she looked up again, the smile had disappeared.

"Like performing a parlor trick, you mean? Reading the cards perhaps."

Although the tone was again *almost* free of inflection, the wording clearly mocked what he'd just asked of her.

"You seem amused by the idea of helping your country."

He sounded like some bureaucratic jerk. Maybe he was,

but there was nothing in the least bit funny to him about what The Covenant was trying to do.

Respect for the old man had caused him to seek this woman out. And it had kept him here, even after he'd learned the truth. Under no other circumstance would he have approached some so-called psychic for help. After what had happened to Gardner, however...

"I'm sorry. I really didn't mean to be flippant. Exactly what do you believe I can do for my country?" The tone of the last was clearly sarcastic, despite her apology.

"I'd ask that what I'm about to tell you remain in strictest confidence."

She lifted one hand as if to indicate their surroundings. "Just who do you think I might tell?"

"I'd like your word that you won't tell *anyone*."

Again the corners of her mouth quirked and were then controlled. She was openly making fun of him. And since Ethan wasn't accustomed to being a source of amusement, it made him uncomfortable.

Granted, he had always taken his responsibilities, both with the agency and then later with the Phoenix, very seriously. Maybe too seriously. That didn't ease the spurt of anger he felt at her unspoken ridicule.

He wondered if he were overreacting because she was a woman. A woman who in any other circumstances he would have been attracted to.

The admission was surprising, but once he'd made it, he realized how accurate it was. Physically, everything about her appealed to him. It was only the other that made him uncomfortable.

"Then you have it, of course." She folded her hands together in her lap again and leaned forward as if eager to hear what he had to say.

The pose didn't fool him. Nor did it mitigate his anger.

He hadn't come here to be mocked. Not about something that was an integral part of who and what he was—

The realization was sudden. And stunning.

As soon as he had realized what she'd done at the CIA, *he* had expected to be amused at any claims *she* would make about her abilities. She had very neatly turned the tables on him instead. Deliberately giving him a dose of his own medicine? he wondered.

He'd been careful not to reveal his skepticism that her "gifts" could prove useful. Careful neither by word nor tone to indicate that he would have walked out immediately after learning about them except for the old man's confidence in her and what had happened two nights ago. So unless she was prescient—

Again, the natural conclusion of that train of thought surprised him. He glanced up, meeting clear green eyes, and found that, although her face was completely controlled, they were full of laughter. As if she knew exactly what he'd been thinking.

It was both disconcerting and annoying. He wasn't accustomed to being manipulated, yet that was exactly how he felt. As if she were the one conducting the interview. As if she were the one making the evaluation.

As if she had found him wanting.

"You were about to tell me about the needs of my country, Mr. Snow," she prodded at his silence.

He took a breath, trying to gather his wits. He had to balance his innate distrust of everything Raine McAllister represented with the very real concerns he had about national security if The Covenant wasn't stopped.

And, too, there was his respect for Montgomery Gardner's judgment. If the old man was right—if it was remotely possible this woman *could* help—then he had an obligation to pursue this.

"We have reason to believe that members of The Covenant are funding, if not actively carrying out, domestic terrorism. We believe they are doing so in an attempt to provoke a response from our government against not only the known terrorist groups, but against the entire Muslim world. To set off an American *jihad*, if you will."

That was the word Bertha Reynolds had used during the final confrontation with Phoenix agent John Edmonds. *Jihad*. Holy war.

"The agency I work for," Ethan continued, choosing his words with care, "had some success several months ago in identifying a few individuals involved in that plan. At the time we were hopeful they were the only members of The Covenant who were in on the plot. That their actions were an aberration in an otherwise legitimate and benign charitable foundation."

When he glanced up, he realized that she was listening intently. At least she was no longer making fun of him.

"Recently," he went on, thinking about the most telling evidence they'd gathered, "there have been at least two bombing attempts that we believe may be tied to the organization. The problem is we can't prove any of this. They've taken great pains to ensure that their membership list remains secret. We've had no success identifying their leaders. Then…Mr. Gardner suggested you could help."

"And now that you know *why* he suggested that?"

Ethan had a feeling that if he attempted to prevaricate, she'd see right through him. Maybe literally.

"My first inclination would be to discount the possibility. I'm not sure I have that option any longer."

Her head tilted, questioning what he'd just said.

"Less than twenty-four hours after he gave me your name, Mr. Gardner was attacked in his home."

"*Attacked?*"

That, at least, was something she hadn't known. There was a fleeting sense of satisfaction until he remembered the seriousness of the old man's condition.

"In an upscale Virginia neighborhood that has one of the lowest crime rates in the nation. Nothing was taken from the house although there were a multitude of valuable objects around. In short, there was no sign that what happened was anything other than a personal attack."

"He isn't dead."

It hadn't sounded like a question, but he answered as if it had been. "He's in critical condition. Given his age…"

There was a long pause. Her eyes, locked on his face, had lost any tendency to laughter.

"And you believe someone did that because you'd gone to talk to him."

"Given the timing, it makes sense."

"Because you talked about *me?*"

"Or about the organization we've been tracking. I've no doubt that I've asked enough questions during the last few months to make them suspicious. Maybe they followed me there. Or it may be that Mr. Gardner was targeted because of his ties to the agency I work for."

The crease he'd noticed before formed again between her brows. "The CIA?"

"A private investigative agency."

"But…" Her lips closed over the question.

"Run by someone who *also* had very close ties to the CIA."

"A private agency? You said your investigation was driven by national security concerns."

"You don't have to be a government operative to want to protect this country and its people from further acts of terrorism."

"But you *were,*" she said. "A government operative."

"At one time."

He didn't elaborate. He wasn't willing to discuss why he had left the CIA.

It had had nothing to do with the disbanding of Cabot's elite counterterrorism team. Ethan had left on his own almost a year before that edict against the External Security Team had come down. And only at the urging of someone he respected as much as he respected Griff Cabot would he ever have become involved in clandestine operations again.

"But he *will* be all right, won't he?"

She meant Gardner, he realized.

Your guess is as good as mine. That answer was no less mocking than some of those she'd made to his appeal. He didn't offer it, however.

Despite his distaste for almost everything he had learned about Raine McAllister, he couldn't shake the notion that he owed it to the old man to treat her, and this entire bizarre episode, with at least some degree of respect. Professional courtesy for a former DCI? Or guilt over the possibility that his and Griff's visit had played a role in the attack that had injured Montgomery Gardner?

"From what everyone says he's a tough old bird," he hedged.

"You don't know him?"

"Not really. I've only met Mr. Gardner a few times. Mostly on social occasions at the home of the owner of the agency, Griff Cabot, and his wife."

She smiled. "As a child, I was always *so* jealous."

It took him a second to make the connection. "Of Claire?"

"She was his granddaughter. We're about the same age. And she had a right to his time and his interest."

Which she had wanted for herself?

"I always wondered if she knew about me," Raine continued. "And if so, exactly what she knew."

"I don't understand."

He didn't. Not her relationship with the old man or her remarks about being jealous of his granddaughter.

"After it was over…" She paused, her eyes again seeming to contemplate a time other than the present. "He paid for my schooling. First, at a very fine girls' boarding school in Virginia, and then later at Wellesley." Her eyes lifted to Ethan's. "I'm afraid I didn't fit very well at either. I always thought Claire would have."

There was no doubt about that, Ethan acknowledged, remembering the poised and beautiful woman who had married Griff Cabot when he'd literally come back from the dead. Despite the very real ideological differences each had brought to that union, theirs seemed to be one of the most successful marriages he'd ever seen.

"When do you want to leave?"

Raine's question, totally out of context in their discussion of Claire Cabot, caught him off guard.

"I beg your pardon?"

"Or were you just planning to point to some names in a copy of *Who's Who?*"

He'd been doing better in the role of stiff-necked bureaucrat, he realized. Playing straight man to her mockery wasn't nearly so appealing.

"You're coming to Washington," he attempted to clarify.

"I thought that's what you wanted."

He had come expecting to be provided with information that would give him a handle on the inner circle of The Covenant. It was obvious now that was something this woman didn't possess. What she did have was a supposed psychic ability Monty Gardner believed in strongly enough to have sent him down here.

And now, because she thought she owed the old man something or maybe because she considered him something of a father figure, she was offering to use her "gift" to help Ethan break the code of silence surrounding the dark heart of an organization he'd spent the past six months investigating. The problem was, no matter what the old man believed about her abilities, Ethan himself didn't think she was capable of doing anything like that.

"I don't—" he began and then stopped. "Actually, I hadn't thought that far."

Back to idiotic straight man, trying to come up with some way of letting her perform her mumbo-jumbo that didn't involve hauling her back to D.C. He didn't even want to think about how her act would be greeted by the hard-nosed ex-intelligence agents of the Phoenix.

"I'll try not to embarrass you, Mr. Snow. I promise you that I've learned a great deal since my Tarot-reading days. And I'd really like to see him," she added softly, her voice more subdued than it had been at any time during the course of their conversation. "It might be my last chance to tell him how much he's always meant to me."

"Of course," Ethan said.

No matter the fallout from this, he realized, given his guilt over the timing of that attack, there really was nothing else he could say to that particular appeal.

RAINE SLIPPED THE CHAIN into the slot on the front door and turned the dead bolt. Normally, despite the isolation of the house, she never thought about those precautions. With all that had happened tonight, she did them automatically.

As soon as she heard the sound of the car's engine kick over, she turned off the outside lights. She stood a moment in the darkness, listening as Ethan Snow backed his car out of her driveway and onto the two-lane, blacktopped beach road.

When the noise of his automobile had faded into the distance, she retraced her steps to the back of the house.

The studio was exactly as she had left it, the figure of the runner still draped under its cloth covering.

For a moment she avoided looking at it, allowing her eyes to move around the room instead, focusing briefly on the completed sculptures. Trying again to find the peace this place had always given her.

Despite her avoidance of the statue that had precipitated the vision, that peace still eluded her. Moving decisively, she crossed the room, intending to uncover the runner. As she approached the figure, however, her steps slowed, almost without her conscious volition.

Although she took a fortifying breath as soon as she reached the pedestal, she didn't allow any other hesitation. She quickly lifted the cloth, revealing the sculpture.

There was no repetition of what had occurred at sunset. Nothing at all unusual happened.

The flowing lines of the figure seemed as pleasing to her as they had last night. Proportioned. Graceful. Displaying exactly the strength and athleticism she'd been trying for.

She circled the stand, examining the statue from every angle. When she reached the front, for almost the first time since she'd shaped the features, she looked at the runner head-on.

Her heart seemed to falter before it resumed beating, but at an increased rate. Although she moved closer, there was no doubt at all about what her eyes had told her.

The straining face of the runner she had fashioned two days ago, the figure that had metamorphosed into the vision of that dark, bottomless pond, was clearly that of the man with whom she had just agreed to travel to Washington tomorrow.

Chapter Three

Ethan almost didn't recognize her. And when he did, he realized he had again misjudged her.

Despite the size and regional flavor of the local airport, she had dressed in a two-piece cotton knit dress in a deep shade of turquoise. The color set off her tanned skin and dark hair. Although she was wearing sandals, they had low heels and matched the calfskin purse slung over her shoulder. A black wheeled suitcase stood beside her.

She watched his approach, her expression unrevealing. Her eyes, which he had thought last night were the color of the sea far out from shore, today seemed to match the vibrant fabric of her dress.

"Ready?" he asked.

He wasn't sure why Raine McAllister seemed capable of reducing him to a degree of social ineptitude he hadn't suffered since high school. Maybe it had something to do with the directness of her gaze.

Or with the fact that she had managed to make him feel last night as if she knew what he was thinking. A formidable obstacle to overcome, even for someone who professed not to believe that was possible.

Considering what he'd been feeling as he'd walked toward her, that wasn't the only obstacle he faced. He had acknowledged his attraction last night when she'd been barefooted, dressed in cutoff jeans, her face devoid of makeup. Today she looked as sophisticated as any of the women he'd encountered during his forays into Washington society.

He could only hope his physical reaction wasn't obvious. And that she couldn't *really* read his mind.

"What time is the flight?" Raine asked.

Obviously her abilities didn't extend to anything as mundane as flight schedules, Ethan thought. A cheap shot maybe, but he was still uncomfortable with this entire scenario. Since he'd pulled out of her driveway last night, he'd been trying to shake off the feeling that agreeing to take Raine back to Washington had been a huge mistake.

When he called Griff to explain why Gardner had recommended they contact her, as well as to warn him that she'd be accompanying him back to D.C. today, he'd learned that Gardner's condition was still listed as critical. Both Griff and Claire were staying at the hospital almost around the clock. So if Raine was determined to see the old man before—

He blocked the unpleasant thought. "How about now?"

Her eyes widened, but she didn't ask any questions. Ethan shifted the strap of his overnight bag to his shoulder and then reached down to take the handle of her suitcase. Without thinking, he put his free hand on the small of her back, intending to direct her toward the door that led out to where the plane was being prepared.

She jumped at his touch, as if a spark of electricity had been conducted from his body to hers. Considering the terrazzo tile floor, that was highly unlikely.

"This way," he said, careful this time not to allow his hand to make contact with her waist.

Pulling her case behind him, he led the way down the

portable steps and onto the tarmac. The Lear, the Phoenix's latest purchase and highly tangible evidence of the agency's success, gleamed sleek and white in the morning sun.

He stopped at the foot of the stairway to glance behind him. Raine was still standing at the top, one hand gripping the railing, her eyes locked on the plane.

"Is something wrong?"

He should have told her they would be taking a private jet. There had been no reason not to. Nothing beyond some kind of perverse attempt to test her abilities, perhaps.

At his question her eyes left the aircraft to focus on his. "We're not flying commercial?"

"I brought the agency's plane down to speed things up."

Both he and Griff had agreed that the attack on the old man had implications for the investigation. If Gardner believed Raine could help, then the quicker Ethan talked to her the better.

"*You're* the pilot?"

"Is that a problem?"

She shook her head, but her gaze fastened again on the jet. Her lips tightened before she looked away. She took another breath, deep enough to be visible, but finally she started down the stairs.

"I'm fully certified," he said when she stepped onto the tarmac beside him. "I have as many hours in the air as most commercial pilots. The plane's new—"

She shook her head again. "It isn't that."

If she's about to come up with some kind of psychic nonsense about why we shouldn't make this flight...

"Then what is it?" His question sounded more abrupt than he'd intended.

"Nothing. I'm ready whenever you are, Mr. Snow."

She headed resolutely toward the plane as if that dramatic pause at the top of the stairs had never occurred.

Except it had. And for some ridiculous reason, it bothered him.

He was aware that there were storms in the area. Their flight plan would take them on a course parallel to them, but far enough away that they shouldn't have any problems. Like any good pilot, he didn't take risks with the weather. And he had always felt safer flying than driving, especially around the Washington area. Now, however...

Unmoving, he watched Raine climb the stairs to the Lear. Just before she stepped through the hatch, she turned to look down at him.

Her glance had been just that. A meeting of the eyes, over before he could decide what he had seen in hers.

The same mockery that had been there last night? Had that hesitation at the top of the stairs been an attempt to rattle him because he didn't believe Gardner's faith in her abilities was justified?

If so, she was in for a surprise, he vowed. It would be a cold day in hell before he bought into any of that palmreading, Tarot-scanning sideshow. A very cold day.

IN STARK CONTRAST to the subtropical sunshine they'd left, Washington was gray and rainy. Maybe the weather was appropriate for the visit they were making, Ethan decided as he led Raine down the corridor of the hospital.

There was only one intensive care waiting room. Through its glass-topped door, he spotted Griff and Claire sitting side by side. They weren't conversing, but they were holding hands, the strain of the vigil they kept etched on their faces.

He opened the door, ushering Raine through. As Griff rose to meet them, Ethan wondered what the head of the Phoenix had told his wife about her grandfather and the woman beside him. Of course, it was always possible Claire had already known about the little girl who had once been so jealous of her relationship with Monty Gardner.

"Ethan," Griff said, and then turned to smile at Raine.

"Raine McAllister, this is Griff Cabot. He's the head of the Phoenix Agency. Mr. Gardner is—"

"I know," she said, holding out her hand. "I'm very glad to meet you, Mr. Cabot."

Griff's eyes met Ethan's briefly before he took the slim fingers in his own. "Griff. And thank you for coming."

"How is he?"

"Holding his own. How much longer he can do that..."

"As long as he has to," Monty Gardner's granddaughter said.

They turned to find that Claire was standing slightly behind her husband. She took another step, entering the triangle the three of them had formed, and held out her hand to Raine.

"I'm Claire Cabot. I understand you know my grandfather."

"I *knew* him," Raine corrected as she took the hand Claire extended. "A very long time ago."

"I see," Claire said after a moment, but it was clear from her tone that she didn't.

"Raine worked with your grandfather," Ethan began, and then wondered whether this was the time or the place to go into exactly what she had done for the CIA.

"With *Grandfather?* But..." It was obvious that, just as he had last night, Claire was trying to make Raine's age fit with the time Montgomery Gardner had been in a position to employ anyone. "I'm afraid I don't understand."

"Raine was a little girl. The agency—"

There was no way to sugarcoat what the CIA had done or Gardner's role in it. Despite her grandfather's position as the director of central intelligence, Claire was not a fan of the agency. The idea of a child like Raine being exploited there would trouble her, just as it had him. And right now he didn't want to say anything that might seem critical of her grandfather.

"Mr. Gardner was very kind to me," Raine said, easing the awkward pause. "In a way that no one else in my life had ever been before."

"I see," Claire said again.

This time her tone seemed even more distant. She was probably trying to figure out why this stranger had intruded at what she must fear might be her grandfather's death bed.

I was always so insanely jealous…. She was his grand-daughter. She had a right to his time and his interest.

Was that why Raine had been so determined to come? Because she was still jealous? Ethan wondered. Except that didn't fit the impression he'd gotten when she'd talked about the old man.

Of course, his assessment hadn't necessarily been made by either his logic or his training. Something far more primitive, more physical than cerebral perhaps, drove his desire to believe she'd had no ulterior motives in coming here.

"You didn't know about me, did you?" Raine asked.

"Know *what* about you?"

There was a hint of arrogance in Claire's question, which might be the result of tiredness or of strain. Of course, it was understandable that Griff's wife wasn't reacting with her usual poise and kindness. To be fearful of losing her grandfather and then to be introduced to a strange woman who claimed to have a long acquaintance with someone to whom she had always been very close…

"It doesn't matter," Raine said. "I just thought he might have mentioned me."

Claire's lips parted as if she wanted to continue her questions. Before she did, however, she glanced at Griff. The small negative movement of his head caused her to close her mouth without another comment.

Ethan wondered which of them Griff was trying to protect—his wife or Raine or maybe even Ethan's investigation. He couldn't believe the very pragmatic head of the Phoenix actually thought Raine McAllister might make a difference in the investigation, so Griff's decision to put an end to this increasingly awkward conversation must have been personal rather than professional.

"I'd like to see him." Raine's voice was properly subdued, considering the circumstances, but she sounded as if she thought that request to be reasonable.

"You want to see my *grandfather?*" Claire obviously couldn't believe what she'd just heard. "Do you have *any* idea—"

"He's only allowed one visitor per hour. On the hour," Griff intervened. "And for only ten minutes."

"That would be more than enough time," Raine said. "Any time at all, actually—"

"Only family is allowed in the room," Claire snapped, making no pretense of politeness this time.

Raine smiled at her, apparently willing to overlook her rudeness. "You've had him your entire life, Claire. Surely you can spare me ten minutes."

"Just who the *hell* do you think you are?" Claire finally exploded, her face flushed and angry.

"His daughter," Raine said.

THE CALM BEEP of the monitors and the low light of the glass-walled cubicle were soothing after the tenseness of the scene in the waiting room. She should have been able to handle that better, Raine thought. Despite the number of times she had tried to imagine a meeting with her father's family, nothing had gone as she'd expected.

She was genuinely sorry to have caused Claire more distress, but she hadn't seen any other way to respond to what she believed was her father's convoluted method of reaching out to her.

When it had become clear Claire was determined to keep someone who had been a mere employee from seeing her grandfather, Raine had felt she had no other choice than to claim her rightful place at his side. And, of course, it would all have to come out eventually.

She supposed she should be thankful Claire's mother hadn't been here. If it was that difficult to learn that you had an aunt you'd never known about, how much more startling would it be to discover the existence of a half sister? One that no one had bothered to tell you about. Not even your father.

She forced her eyes away from the digital display to watch the even rise and fall of Montgomery Gardner's chest. The ventilator breathed for him, its slow rhythm almost mesmerizing.

She stepped nearer the bed as the nurse pulled the curtain closed to give them a modicum of privacy. For a moment the features of the man in the narrow, railed bed were unfamiliar. Almost alien.

Not only were the tubes and wires distracting, the signs of the attack he'd suffered were brutally clear. Blood had pooled beneath the thin skin under his eyes, blackening both of them. The gash on his forehead had been neatly stitched, but it was long and swollen.

She resisted the urge to touch his cheek, putting her hand on the top of his wrist instead. His skin was cool and dry.

Too cool? she wondered, but the steady blip of the monitor reassured that sudden fear.

He was holding his own, Cabot had said. And he would, as long as he has to, his granddaughter had added.

In spite of those determinedly optimistic evaluations, the old man's strength was nearly at an end. Raine had known that, as far away as she had been. Throughout today's journey she had sensed that he was almost too tired to fight anymore. So very tired of it all, she thought, running her fingers along his forearm, which was nothing but skin and bones.

Maybe that's why he had sent for her after all these years. Because he was tired of seeing everything he had devoted his life to endangered. He wouldn't have told them that, of course. He would never reveal that much of himself or his feelings.

Instead, he had dispatched Ethan Snow with the suggestion that she could help if they would contact her. And at one time that might even have been true. Now, however...

"Why didn't you send for me before?" she whispered, bending to put her mouth near his ear.

There was no reaction. His eyelids, their thin blue veins visible beneath the fragile skin, never moved.

All these years she had waited, respecting his wishes. Until today she had never demanded his attention, never approached any member of his family, never interfered with their lives in any way.

For a year after his wife's death, which she had read about in the papers, she had waited for him to call, believing that now he would finally acknowledge her existence. Apparently he'd decided that would still be too traumatic for the remaining members of his family. Judging by Claire's reaction, he had been right.

She was sorry she'd broken the news so abruptly. Cruelly, she admitted, but she truly believed her father wanted to see her. If he hadn't, why would he have given Ethan Snow her name?

Besides, if she hadn't revealed their relationship, his

family would never have allowed her into this room. If the doctors were right, and there really was so little time...

She bent closer, her lips parted to speak to him again, and discovered she didn't know what to call him. She had never called him "Father." Not aloud. Yet to call him "Mr. Gardner" seemed a denial of all that he had meant in her life.

"I don't know that I can help your friends. So many things have happened..." She hesitated. That wasn't something she wanted to share with him. Not now. "But I'll try."

For a moment Ethan Snow's face was in her mind's eye, his voice passionate, touchingly sincere, as he talked about protecting his country.

Her father shared that same patriotism and dedication. That's what he had asked of her before. That's all he was asking now. And she would do the very best she could, despite what had happened in the past.

"I promise you I'll try."

This time she leaned forward to press her lips against the undamaged side of his forehead. As soon as they made contact with the old man's skin, the nearly electric force that had caused the statue of the runner to morph into something else jolted through her consciousness again.

The image was exactly the same. Dark water. Cold and deep and still. And somehow deadly.

Aware this time of what might happen, she instantly began to fight against its pull. She jerked her eyes open and stumbled backwards, bumping into a monitor and sending it rolling away from the bed.

It had been attached to one of the myriad wires, of course. As the connection was disrupted, an alarm sounded, loud and demanding in the quietness.

The curtain behind her was thrown open, and two nurses

rushed in. One of them began to adjust the monitor she'd stumbled into, thankfully silencing the alarm, while the other went over to examine their patient.

"I'm sorry," Raine said. "I backed into one of the machines, and it went off. Nothing's wrong with my father. It was just an accident."

The nurse by the bed looked over her shoulder. "You'll have to leave."

"But I told you—"

"I'm sorry. You can wait in the waiting room. Someone will call you."

The nurse who had readjusted the monitor took her by the elbow, directing her toward the curtain.

"Come on, my dear. Better to get out of the way so we can make sure everything is all right."

She wanted that, of course, but she had the feeling that if she let them send her away, she would never be allowed to return. There were too many things left unsaid.

And too many years during which they might have been said. On both sides.

The drape was pulled closed behind her, and Raine found herself standing alone in front of the cubicle. She thought about waiting out here until they were through, but one of the other RNs from the nurses' station rose and started toward her.

Raine put her purse over her shoulder and looked at the glass door leading out of the ICU unit. A man waited beside it, his eyes directed not inside, but at the white tile wall opposite him. He stood with his arms crossed in front of his body, the left holding the wrist of the right.

He wore a gray, three-button suit over a white dress shirt and blue tie. His salt-and-pepper hair had been cut almost militarily short, and he was clean shaven. Although she had never seen him before, the look was one she instantly recognized, despite the passage of years. Perhaps the style of the suit had changed, but the way he was dressed was what she had once considered to be the agency's unofficial uniform.

Another of Cabot's men? Assigned to protect her father? Or assigned to watch her?

That was possible. Cabot and Ethan Snow were probably already in the process of trying to verify her claim.

Other than asking the man in the cubicle behind her, she wasn't sure how they would do that. Monty Gardner was far too adept at keeping secrets. After all, he had had more than forty years with the CIA to perfect the art.

"I think it would be better if you go back to the waiting room now," the nurse from the station said.

Startled from her contemplation of the man outside, Raine turned to smile at her. "Of course. You *will* send for me when they've checked out the equipment, won't you? I wasn't in there but a minute or two. I'd really appreciate another chance to talk to my father."

The nurse looked slightly taken aback, perhaps because of Gardner's physical condition. It was obvious that any conversation wouldn't be two-way.

"I'm sure there'll be other opportunities," she said. "Now, if you don't mind…" The nurse gestured toward the exit to the unit.

Given no choice, Raine walked across the room and pushed the bar that would release the door. As it opened with a pneumatic hiss, the eyes of the man who had been waiting outside met hers.

"Ms. McAllister?"

He had obviously been given her description. Maybe he had a message from Ethan or the Cabots.

"Yes?"

"If you'd come with me, ma'am." He took a step along the corridor as if her consent would be automatic.

"Come with you where?"

He turned back, smiling at her. Although it was an attractive smile, it didn't quite reach his eyes, which she saw were an unusual shade of brown, so light they were almost gold.

"To rejoin your party, of course."

Ethan? Or the Cabots?

The latter seemed unlikely, given Claire's reaction. Maybe Ethan had arranged for her to be escorted to somewhere besides the waiting room, so that she and Claire wouldn't meet again.

"And I need an escort to do that?" she asked.

The man's smile widened before it became a soft chuckle. Even his laughter didn't change the amber eyes.

"I'm just following orders, Ms. McAllister."

That, too, was something she remembered from when she was a child. That's what they all said. All those hard men had always just been following orders.

All but my father, who gave them.

As the charge nurse had done inside the ICU, her escort put out his hand, gesturing down the hallway. Raine glanced back through the glass door, but the curtain around her father's cubicle was still closed.

They had said they'd send for her, but they would assume she had returned to the waiting room. If Ethan were waiting for her somewhere else and she allowed this man to take her there, they wouldn't know where to find her.

"I'll have to tell the nurses where I'll be."

When she turned back, the man was no longer smiling. His eyes seemed even more golden. Lighter. Colder.

Colder?

"I'll send someone to tell them," he said, taking her arm.

She was getting tired of people doing that, she realized. As if they thought she wasn't capable of making up her own mind about where she wanted to go. She pulled against his hold, but instead of releasing her, his fingers tightened painfully around her elbow.

"What do you think you're doing?"

She hadn't finished the sentence before he'd pulled her against him, her back to his chest. Something hard was pressed into the base of her spine. For a second or two she didn't understand its significance. Not until he put his cheek next to hers, his mouth close to her ear.

"Walk," he said. "Don't look back. Don't talk. Just walk. I'll tell you where."

When she didn't move, more out of shock than from any intention to resist, the object in her back, which she now realized must be the muzzle of a gun, ground into her backbone. He closed the distance between them, which had the effect of both hiding the weapon and, at the same time, urging her forward.

"I don't know how much you know about firearms, Ms. McAllister, but the one at your back is a 9 mm. Trust me when I tell you it will blow a very big hole in your spine."

She did trust what he'd just said. Just as she knew he would have no compunction in pulling the trigger.

It was damned late to be getting that kind of clear message about what was happening, she thought. Far too late to do her any good.

From the first she had tried to tell Ethan Snow that she couldn't help him, but he hadn't listened. And then when she had heard Monty Gardner was involved, she had put her doubts aside in order to make this journey.

One that was a waste of everyone's time. Because now she had absolute proof that she couldn't even use her gift to help herself.

Chapter Four

"She said *nothing* about Gardner being her father, I swear to you," Ethan said for the second or third time. "She told me she'd worked for him. That he'd paid for her to go to school—a finishing school of some kind—and then to college. If I'd had any idea that she would say something like that to Claire, I swear I'd never have brought her here."

In all the years that Ethan had known him, he'd seen very few things rattle Griff Cabot. Anything that affected the well-being of his family was obviously one of them.

Although he hadn't been in on the action, Ethan knew that the Phoenix had been born out of a dangerous operation Griff's former External Security Team members had undertaken, at Cabot's request, to rescue his daughter from a kidnapper. The fact that Griff had blown the cover the CIA had arranged for him in order to carry out that mission indicated exactly where his priorities lay.

"I think she's lying," Cabot said curtly. "I've known Monty Gardner a long time, both before and after I met Claire. There's never been a man more devoted to his family."

"Maybe after his wife died—"

"He's been a widower for less than seven years. It won't

wash, Ethan. Whatever Raine McAllister is selling, I'm not buying.''

Despite his sympathy for Claire, who had clearly been distraught, for some reason Ethan felt compelled to defend Raine against that characterization.

''I'm not sure she's selling *anything*. She hasn't made any claims on Gardner's estate or on the family. At least, not yet. I think she just wanted to see the old man again. It may be that when she was told visitation was for family only—''

''She dreamed up that story about being his daughter?'' Griff interrupted. ''That's even *more* unforgivable. Besides, a claim like that is too easy to disprove. She has to know she can't get away with this.''

''Maybe she only needed to get away with it tonight.''

''You think she wants access to his room to do him harm?''

As the thought occurred to him, Griff started toward the corridor leading to the ICU. And considering the seemingly inexplicable attack on Gardner, that suspicion wasn't as farfetched as it normally would have been.

Ethan grabbed his arm, forcibly restraining him. ''I'm not suggesting anything like that. We've all been afraid he won't make it. She was, too. She wanted to see him before it was too late. Maybe she was desperate enough to come up with that story.''

Claire had vehemently denied her claim, but Raine had been resolute that she was Gardner's daughter. And equally resolute in her demand that she be allowed to see her grandfather. She hadn't wavered from either position, not even in the face of Claire's escalating anger. When Griff had taken his wife out of the waiting room to calm down, Raine had taken the opportunity to present herself to the ICU staff as Gardner's daughter, newly arrived from out of town.

Given the Cabots' explanation about the manner under which the unit allowed visitation, Ethan had expected her request to see him to be turned down. It hadn't been. She'd been ushered inside the ICU unit before Griff's return.

At least Claire had no idea as yet that Raine had been allowed in to see her grandfather. As exhausted and as anxious as she was, that would probably have been the last straw.

"I don't care how desperate *she* is," Griff said. "I won't have her adding to his family's stress."

"*Gardner* gave us her name. That means there's some—"

"He provided her name as someone who could help the investigation. *Not* as his illegitimate daughter."

"Maybe not, but there's *some* bond between them that's important to them both. After all, he paid for her education. And that's the only reason she let me in, by the way. Because I told her Gardner was a mutual friend."

"I'm willing to believe she cares for him. About him," Griff amended. "The other, however—"

"Mr. Gardner's daughter? You may come back to the ICU now."

They turned to find the nurse who'd just made that announcement standing in the door of the waiting room.

"She's already in the ICU," Ethan offered.

"The pretty brunette?"

An apt description, Ethan thought. Of course, he'd already admitted his bias in that respect.

"She went in maybe ten minutes ago."

"But we sent her back out," the nurse said, coming over to them. "There was a problem with one of the monitors. She was going to come here and wait until it was resolved."

Automatically Ethan scanned the faces of the people

gathered in the room, although he would surely have noticed if she'd returned. Raine was definitely not among them.

"Maybe she decided to wait in the corridor," he suggested.

"But…I just came that way. There's no one there."

"Maybe she left," Griff said, his voice hard. It was obvious that as far as he was concerned, that would be nothing but good riddance, despite the static state of the Phoenix's investigation.

"She seemed very anxious to visit her father," the nurse said, peering around the room as if she thought they might have missed her. "I can't imagine where she's gotten off to."

Uneasiness stirred in Ethan's stomach. If Raine wasn't in the waiting room or in the corridor…

"I'll help you look," he offered.

"Of course, she *could* come back during the next regular visitation time," the nurse said, apparently ready to give up the search as too time consuming in the face of her other duties.

"Not if I can help it," Griff said under his breath.

"I'm sorry?" The nurse appeared puzzled by the comment.

"There are some…family tensions."

Ethan doubted Griff would appreciate his explanation, but maybe it would be better if the staff understood that Gardner's relatives weren't pleased about sharing the precious few minutes they had to visit him with someone they viewed as an imposter.

"Is there a ladies' room nearby?" Ethan asked.

"Of course. Why didn't I think of that? She was upset when the alarm sounded."

The nurse continued to talk as she led the way back to

the waiting room door, Ethan following. He'd leave it to Griff to explain the situation to Claire.

He only hoped the two women hadn't chosen the same rest room in which to attempt repair to their shattered emotions. When the nurse searched the one nearest the ICU, however, she found it was empty.

"Maybe she decided to go down for coffee," she said. "If you see her, would you tell her that her father is still the same. And that she was right. The problem was in the machine."

"I'll tell her," Ethan promised.

He watched as the woman walked down the corridor and pressed the button that would give her admittance to the ICU. Standing there alone, he couldn't shake the feeling that something was wrong.

Raine had been determined to see the old man. If her visit had been cut short, then she should have been waiting around here to be readmitted.

Except she wasn't. Knowing how furious Claire had been about the idea of letting her in to see her grandfather, he didn't believe Raine would risk the family taking steps to prevent her from doing that again.

Claire's departure from the waiting room had been her window of opportunity. He couldn't see her giving it up to go down to the cafeteria for coffee.

And if not, then where the hell was she?

THERE HAD BEEN NO HESITATION in the gunman's guidance. He was obviously very familiar with the hospital or he had explored this route before he'd come to wait for her outside the ICU.

As she'd followed his directions down the dingy, narrow corridors of a part of the building obviously frequented only by staff and maintenance, Raine had thought they would surely encounter someone. If they did, she planned to try to signal to them that she needed help.

The only people they'd passed, however, had been a couple of nurses, who hurried by them with their eyes downcast. Tellingly, they had both been carrying purses.

Coming in to work from the parking deck? If so, that must where her captor was taking her.

If this were like the parking facilities of most hospitals, it would be filled with cars and people at this time of day. He probably wouldn't be willing to use the gun out there among them. That wasn't a given, of course, but she thought a more likely scenario was that he would put her into whatever vehicle he'd driven here and take her with him.

The crucial questions were why he wanted to do that and where he intended to take her—neither of which she could answer. She couldn't begin to speculate on what this abduction might be about—other than the Phoenix's investigation, which also seemed to have precipitated the attack on her father.

Someone obviously believed the two of them knew something about the organization Ethan Snow had mentioned. Maybe her father did, but if so, why hadn't he given that information to Ethan and Cabot when he had the chance?

As for her, she knew nothing about The Covenant. She couldn't remember hearing the name before Ethan had mentioned it in her living room last night.

''To the left,'' the man behind her directed.

His hold on her arm hadn't loosened, nor had the muzzle of the weapon he held shifted. As they walked, she could feel it rubbing against her spine.

''Punch the up button,'' he instructed as they approached a bank of three elevators.

As soon as they were in front of the doors of the first, she obeyed, reaching out to push the ascending arrow. The sign on the wall listed a color match for each parking level, four of which were above the floor they were on.

This might be her last chance, Raine realized, especially if he had parked on the top level, which in any deck was apt to be sparsely populated. The last opportunity to effect an escape before he got her alone.

If there's someone inside when the doors open—

Two chimes signaled the near-simultaneous arrival of two separate cars. Still without any clear-cut plan, she tensed, preparing to take whatever opportunity presented itself.

Would he shoot me in cold blood with a witness present?

Her sense from the first had been that he would. Certainly if he was pushed.

If she was right about that, as soon as he got her into a deserted area, then he would kill her. But if he'd been instructed to take her somewhere instead of killing her here—

The doors of the elevator in front of her, as well as the ones on the one beside it, began to slide open. She took a breath, afraid that if she did anything more to prepare, she would communicate her intent to him.

The opening doors revealed an elderly woman and a man in a wheelchair. The man looked frail, but the woman was tall and raw-boned. Her white uniform seemed to indicate she was the man's caregiver rather than a relative.

"Excuse us, please," the woman said cheerily as she began to maneuver the chair out of the elevator.

Raine and her captor were standing so close it would be difficult for the caregiver to get the chair out around them. Despite that, the man behind Raine made no move to step aside, perhaps fearful that in doing so, he might reveal his weapon.

"Watch your toes, dear," the woman warned as she attempted to roll her charge by them.

Taking advantage of the situation, Raine pretended she was forced to take a step to the side in order to get out of the way of the wheelchair. The move caught her captor by surprise, and the hold on her elbow loosened fractionally.

When it did, she jerked her arm forward as hard as she could. Incredibly, it slipped out of the man's grasp.

She sprinted to the next elevator, whose doors, with perfect timing, began to close as soon as she ran between them. That didn't prevent her from pressing the close-door button when she'd located it.

Outside there was an ungodly commotion. It sounded as if, in pursuing her, her captor had somehow become entangled with the wheelchair, maybe upsetting it. The female aide was shrieking something unintelligible. The man with the gun shouted an obscenity just as the elevator doors slid together.

Heart racing, her breath coming in audible gasps, Raine tried to think what she should do next. If she were right about her captor having deliberately parked at the top of the parking deck...

Frantically she punched the button for the floor below it. Her eyes watched the elevator's climb while she prayed she'd been in time. A soft ping gave the answer to that plea.

As soon as the doors opened, she stepped out and began running full-out down a corridor that looked very much like the one she'd just left. She needed to find another set of elevators or figure out how to get back into the main section of the hospital as quickly as she could.

Once she'd done that, she would think about what came next. She wasn't sure she wanted to go back to the ICU, since that's where the man with the gun had been waiting for her.

And in all probability, it was where he would begin his search for her this time. *If* he were brazen enough to try to take her again.

Of course, the ICU area was also where Ethan Snow was. Despite the fact that he was little more than a stranger, her inclination was to find him as quickly as she could.

He was the ex-CIA agent. He was also the one who had gotten her into this. And beside that, he was—

The sound of a chime from the other end of the corridor put a halt to her list of Ethan Snow's crimes and attributes. The chances that the occupant of that arriving elevator was her captor were remote. Unless…

She tried to picture the elevator bank where she'd pulled off her escape. Had the floors where the elevators stopped been shown above each car? If so, it was possible he'd tracked her by simply watching those numbers flash by until the elevator had stopped on this particular floor.

The spurt of adrenaline produced by that realization pushed her to increase her speed. Breathless, she finally rounded a corner to see a small offset with a double bank of elevators.

She rushed into the center of it, pushing the up and down arrows on both sides repeatedly. Rationally she knew that wouldn't make them arrive any quicker, but she felt she had so little control over what was happening that doing something—even if it were pointless—seemed to help.

The first car to arrive was going down. And it was empty. As she stepped in and pushed the close-door button, she heard what sounded like someone running down the corridor she'd just traversed.

The footsteps were heavy. A man's hard-soled shoes, slamming against the polished tile with each step.

When the elevator doors closed, she leaned, weak and panting, against the cool metal wall before she realized she hadn't made a floor selection. She straightened, looking at the control panel. The only lighted indicator was for the first floor. If she didn't do something soon—

The chime and a soft bump indicated it was too late to change her destination. An upward glance at the numbers above the doors confirmed she had already arrived on the main floor.

Maybe that would be an advantage, she told herself. More people. More protection. Security guards.

The doors opened to reveal none of those things. She was in another offset hallway, the corridor that fronted it as deserted as had been the one she'd just left.

Except for the sound of those running footsteps, she amended.

She shot a look above the elevator she'd just exited, which confirmed her worst fears. The numbers of all the floors were displayed, the *L,* for lobby, now brightly lit.

He would have been able to follow her from floor to floor, so the footsteps she'd heard had undoubtedly been his. Which meant there wasn't a moment to lose. As soon as he could get an elevator, he'd follow her down here, too.

She ran out into the corridor and turned right without taking time to look at the signs on the wall. Her most immediate need was to get away from the elevators. As far away from them as she could before he arrived.

Despite the rather obvious fact that this wasn't a major hallway of the hospital, she passed far more people than she had since she'd made her escape. Not enough to constitute a crowd. Certainly not enough to hide among.

Several stopped and gaped as she ran by. Belatedly she realized that calling attention to herself like this meant that any of them would be able to describe her to her pursuer and tell him exactly which direction she'd been heading.

She slowed to a walk, at the same time trying to ease her ragged breathing. Trying desperately now to blend in with the other visitors.

Suddenly the corridor she'd been following came to an abrupt end. Her two choices were clearly communicated by the arrows on the wall. The one that pointed to the left said Main Lobby. The other indicated that it led to the financial and administrative offices. And the cafeteria.

She hesitated, weighing the advantages and disadvantages of entering either of the most public areas of the hospital. Could they possibly have someone watching the main entrances and exits in case she managed to escape from the man with the gun?

If so, she'd be better off following the arrow that led to the business offices. There would be plenty of exits there. Fire doors if nothing else. And at this point she wasn't averse to setting off some alarms.

She adjusted the strap of her purse more securely over her shoulder, taking a quick look behind her. The man who'd held a gun to her back wasn't behind her. *Not yet at least.*

She turned in the direction leading away from the lobby, walking purposefully down the cross corridor. There were a comforting number of people, most of them probably headed to the cafeteria. The smell of food was tantalizingly close, reminding her that she hadn't eaten anything since breakfast.

She walked past the line of patrons waiting to go in, careful to keep her face turned away from the glass-enclosed serving area. Beyond the relatively crowded entrance lay a broad hall, whose tile floor gleamed empty and inviting.

Business offices. Administration and finance. All she had to do now was to find an outside door—

Just as she congratulated herself on having successfully evaded her pursuer, a masculine hand closed painfully tight around her elbow.

Chapter Five

"Where the hell have you been?"

Ethan. Despite the fury in his question, Raine had to fight the inclination to throw herself into his arms. She couldn't remember responding to any other man like that in her entire life.

Since she'd never been in this situation before, it was hardly surprising that she was relieved not to be confronting her pursuer. What she'd felt when she recognized Ethan, however, went far beyond relief. It encompassed feelings that she would have to reexamine at a time when someone wasn't trying to kill her.

"There was a man..." she began.

Suddenly she realized that her explanation, although necessary, shouldn't take place in this exposed location. She had already turned, trying to draw him down the hallway.

"What man?" he demanded.

"We've got to get out of here."

"What's wrong?"

"Just come on. I'll tell you as soon as—"

The hold on her elbow tightened, pulling her to an abrupt stop. "Tell me now."

His gray eyes were as cold as his tone. And it was obvious he wasn't going to budge until he'd heard at least some of what had happened.

"A man was waiting outside the ICU. He knew my name. He asked me to come with him...." She hesitated, trying to remember exactly how he'd managed to lure her away. "He said he was taking me to rejoin my party. I thought that meant he was taking me to meet you."

"Describe him."

She remembered her first impression of the man who'd been waiting for her. Although she had no proof of what she'd thought then, she blurted it out in her hurry to get Ethan out of the center of the hall.

"I think he was an agent."

"An *agent?*"

"CIA. He *looked* CIA."

For a long heartbeat, Ethan said nothing. "And he tried to take you somewhere."

"He said he was following orders. I refused because I thought the nurses wouldn't know where to find me if I left the area, and that's when he... He had a gun. He said it was a 9 mm, and he put it against the base of my spine..." She was talking too much. Taking too much time to get the explanation out. All she needed to do right now was make him understand the urgency of getting out of this crowded hallway.

"He tried to take me to the parking deck, but I broke away from him. He's following me."

"Now?"

"Unless I lost him. Please come on," she implored, taking his hand to urge him away from the cafeteria.

His gaze focused over her head, examining the corridor behind them. She turned, her eyes following his, and searched the faces of the people behind them.

"You see him?"

Although there was still a mob around the cafeteria entrance, she couldn't spot the man who'd tried to abduct her. "No, but that doesn't mean he isn't back there somewhere."

"Good," Ethan said shortly.

He forced her forward with his hand at the small of her back. And the direction in which he was guiding her was toward the cafeteria.

"What are you doing?" Almost of their own accord, however, her feet had begun to move, carrying her along beside the man who was striding rapidly down the corridor.

"Trying to find whoever's been chasing you."

That response summed up the obvious differences between her and Ethan Snow. She had sense enough to avoid men with guns, especially if they were threatening her with them; he seemed to want to confront them.

"Why in the world would you want—"

"Because that's the only way we're going to find out who he is. Or more importantly, who sent him."

"You think you'll *recognize* him?"

Caught up in his sense of urgency, she was no longer attempting to slow their forward progress. As they approached the line in front of the door to the serving area, her eyes considered the faces of those waiting. The man with the cold, amber eyes wasn't among them.

"If he really is CIA, then I might."

"I don't know that. He just…had that look."

His eyes cut down to her face, despite the fact that he had also been concentrating on the people in the crowd. She looked up to meet them and realized that what she'd just said amused him. He wasn't openly smiling, but the amusement was reflected in his eyes. The expression of emotion she had futilely searched for in the eyes of her captor.

"And yes, you do," she said, deliberately turning to scan a group of people who were approaching the other end of the line.

"I do what?"

"Have that look."

He did. Dark and dangerous. As if he knew his way around the right end of a weapon. On him, however...

"Excuse us," Ethan said, pulling her with him through the mob at the entrance of the cafeteria. "Excuse us, please."

"What are you *doing?*" she protested, smiling apologetically at the family they had just broken in front of.

"We aren't going to be served. There's no point in standing in line."

She closed her lips against any further objections, concentrating on following him through the service area and past the cash registers. Her eyes scanned those seated at the close-packed tables, but there was no sign of the man with the gun.

"This should do."

Ethan was standing beside a table set against the glass wall that separated the cafeteria from the hallway where the line had formed. He had pulled out one of the chairs, holding it as if he were waiting for her to sit down.

"What for?"

"We're going to watch for your guy."

"Here?"

"Why not? It's the perfect view."

He was right. If she were sitting in the chair he held out, she would be able to see anyone approaching this area from the corridor where she'd gotten off the elevators.

And they would be able to see her.

"I can't do this," she said when she realized that.

"All you have to do is identify him."

And I'll handle the rest. That was the implication of his tone at least.

There was a growing pressure in her chest, making it difficult to breathe. She looked at the people seated at the nearby tables. Most of them were family groups, and they included small children.

"You don't understand," she said, remembering those cold, golden eyes.

And remembering her clear impression that he would do exactly what he said he would. If she'd refused to go with him at the ICU, he would have pulled the trigger and blown a hole in her back. If he saw her sitting here in plain sight—

For an instant the noises of people eating and conversing faded from her consciousness to be replaced by the sound of gunshots. Breaking glass. Hysteria.

"Tell me."

Called back from those images of chaos and destruction by Ethan's demand, she realized that his eyes had lost all trace of the amusement she'd seen there only seconds ago.

"He'll shoot. Even in here," she said, crossing her arms over her chest because of the coldness centered there. "He'll fire into this crowd if he sees me. It won't bother him if he hits someone else."

Her eyes left Ethan's face to focus on the towheaded toddler seated in the high chair at the next table. She shivered.

Ethan didn't ask why she believed that. He didn't ask her anything at all.

"If he'd been able to follow me," she reasoned, trying to clear her mind of the grisly pictures that had invaded it, "he would have been here by now. He's probably looking for me in the ICU. Or he's given up. Maybe he left."

"Or maybe he saw me grab you in the hallway."

It took a second or two for her to reach the conclusion he had. "He recognized you?"

"Or he knew *I'd* recognize *him.*"

She couldn't dispute the possibility. She had already acknowledged that in so many ways they were alike. Two sides of the same coin.

Except that whatever had happened to turn the man with the amber eyes into what he had become hadn't changed Ethan Snow. Not at the heart. Not where it mattered.

THANKFULLY ETHAN hadn't parked in the deck when they'd arrived. She wasn't sure she could have borne the thought of having to retrace that journey back to those particular elevators, with their color-coded instructions.

Despite having Ethan by her side, his hand at her waist, she'd been anxious until they had actually climbed into his car and driven away from the hospital. She hadn't been sure if that uneasiness had been caused by residual nerves from her encounter or if the man who had taken her captive still presented a legitimate threat.

Only when Ethan directed the dark-green M-Class he'd picked up at the airport out into the late-afternoon Beltway traffic had she been able to relax. And to try to put the events of the day into some kind of perspective.

"So where are we going?"

"Griff wants to see you."

The tension that had begun to ease built again at the thought of facing Cabot. And more especially Claire. "At his house?"

"At the Phoenix office."

It made sense. Claire's husband wouldn't want her on his home turf. Not if she were likely to run into his wife again.

"I'm sorry I had to do that," Raine said.

"Do what?"

"To tell her like that. So…abruptly. I was afraid that if I didn't, she wouldn't let me see him."

"Your *father?*" His tone was skeptical.

Why wouldn't it be? He had believed almost nothing she'd told him since he'd shown up at her front door last night. His reaction to her warning in the cafeteria had been the sole exception in the course of their short acquaintance.

"He *is* my father."

"I hope you have proof of that."

"Is that what Cabot wants? Proof?"

"For starters."

"He protected his family as long as he could."

"So *you* told them."

"He *sent* for me. There had to be a reason for that."

"I told you why he gave me your name. He thought you could help us with The Covenant."

"It was his way of getting in touch with me. Your asking for his help provided him with an excuse to make contact again."

She didn't understand why after living all these years without her father acknowledging her existence, this had become so important to her. Maybe, as she'd thought from the moment Ethan had broken the news about the attack, because this might be her last chance.

"If that's what he wanted to do," Ethan said, taking his eyes off the road long enough to glance at her, "it would have seemed easier to pick up the phone."

"I don't expect you to understand—"

"Good. Because I don't. What you did back there—" He stopped, taking a slow breath before he continued. "To an outsider, it seemed cruel. And unnecessary."

The accusation hurt, more than she wanted to admit. She

closed her lips, swallowing against the tightness in her throat.

Cruel she would have to accept, especially when she remembered Claire Cabot's face. And she was truly sorry for that. But unnecessary…?

"He's my father," she said, trying not to let any of that emotion show. "And I was afraid I'd never see him again. If you can't understand that…"

She couldn't think of any way to finish that sentence. Ethan's sympathies all seemed to lie with Claire, who had always had everything.

You sound like a child. Still jealous. Still wanting things you can never have.

"I do understand," Ethan said, his voice less judgmental. "It just seemed you could have waited until a less traumatic time to break news like that."

It had been obvious to everyone that Claire was under an enormous amount of stress, and she had added to it. Raine couldn't argue with Ethan's assessment, although it didn't address the fact that she'd been afraid her father was dying. Or that he'd been trying to get in touch with her.

"You told me you were mistreated as a child. I can't believe Mr. Gardner would let something like that happen. Or was that an exaggeration?"

She noticed that he didn't refer to Gardner as her father. Of course, to be fair, she hadn't been completely comfortable using that terminology in the ICU today.

"He didn't know."

"He didn't know you were being beaten?"

"He didn't know anything about me."

"Are you saying he didn't know you were his daughter?"

"My mother didn't tell him. She didn't intend for him to ever know, I think, but… She died when I was four."

It had always bothered her that she could remember so little of her mother. Not even what she looked like. She did remember her perfume. Even now when she smelled anything with those same undertones of jasmine and roses, it brought back an unaccustomed feeling of security. The memory of being loved and cosseted.

And she remembered her voice. Deep and husky, probably from the cigarettes she smoked almost incessantly.

It was as if she had just remembered that her mother smoked, she realized. As if that were something she had forgotten long ago and that had only now, in talking about her, come back to her.

"And then?" Ethan prompted.

"My uncle and aunt took me. My uncle knew who my father was, but he didn't tell him about me. He didn't even tell him that my mother had died."

"If he didn't tell him, then how did Mr. Gardner come to know about you?"

"The agency was looking for people like me. When he saw me, he knew. At least that I was her daughter. The rest was a matter of timing, I suppose. And there were the letters my mother had written to my uncle. I still had those. They were almost all I had left of her."

"You have them now?"

"I think he must have them. My father. I'm not sure where."

"You *do* understand—"

"How preposterous it all sounds?" she challenged. "Maybe I could try to think up some other explanation. Something you and Mr. Cabot won't have any trouble believing."

"Think fast, then," Ethan suggested, as he pulled into the parking lot of an office building which seemed comprised mostly of black glass. On the central door was a discreet graphic of a bird spreading its wings to rise up out of a flame. "I should warn you, however. Griff Cabot isn't someone you want to try and hoodwink. He has far too many resources at his disposal."

While she had none, Raine acknowledged bitterly. Not even, it seemed, the one she'd been born with.

Chapter Six

"I know you don't believe me, but I'd remind you that *you* approached *me*. I've never communicated with any member of Mr. Gardner's family."

Ethan noticed that Raine wasn't referring to the old man as her father. Not in front of Griff. Given Cabot's mood right now, that was probably a wise decision.

"And you never intended to, of course?" Griff said.

"If Ethan hadn't told me about Mr. Gardner's condition, I wouldn't be in Washington right now. I told him from the beginning that I can't help with your investigation."

"But you *did* tell him why Monty Gardner thought you could?"

Griff was in interrogation mode. Ethan had seen him reduce strong men to stammering by those rapid-fire questions. Raine didn't appear to be intimidated.

"I'm sure you know *exactly* what I told him. I'll be glad to repeat it for you, if you like. I took part in CIA experiments during a time when the agency was exploring the possibility of using psychics in intelligence gathering."

"Something called Grill Flame," Griff said.

There was a moment's hesitation. The small furrow Ethan had noticed before had again formed between Raine's brows.

"Cassandra," she said softly, seeming unsure of the name even as she spoke it.

"Cassandra?" Griff's inquiry sounded genuine, in contrast to the sarcastic ones he'd used to solicit information he had already possessed.

"Project Cassandra," Raine said again, sounding more certain this time. "I don't remember anything called Grill Flame. Maybe the others worked on that, but…" She shook her head.

"Monty must have felt you were one of his more successful psychics to recommend you to us."

Cabot had apparently decided to let her comment about the name of the project go unchallenged. Ethan knew him well enough to recognize that he'd been puzzled by it and had undoubtedly filed it away for future reference.

"Since I have no idea how successful the others were, I can't verify that. But because he would almost certainly know that I'm no longer involved in the kind of thing I did for the CIA, I naturally assumed his summons was personal."

"You're suggesting that he was using our investigation as a means to contact you?"

"Sometimes it's hard for men, especially of his generation, to express their emotions. I thought that he was using the work I'd done for the agency as a way to reestablish communication."

"And exactly what kind of work did you do?"

"*They* called it remote viewing. To me it was little more than a game. They showed me a picture or pointed to some place on a map, and I described what was there."

"I understand you have other talents as well. Ones you *didn't* use for the agency."

"I'm not sure what you mean."

"Would it surprise you to learn that your name is well

known in law enforcement circles?'' Griff asked, opening a manila folder that had been lying on the desk in front of him since the interview had begun.

Ethan realized that Cabot had apparently called in some favors between the time he'd left the hospital and tonight's meeting. Or maybe he'd had his operatives begin gathering information on Raine after Ethan's phone call last night. In either case, the file in front of him was impressively thick.

And Ethan found that he didn't want to know what it contained. Not after Cabot's remark about her notoriety among law enforcement.

The possibility that Raine might have been running scams using her supposed psychic abilities made him sick at his stomach. It also made him aware of how far he'd strayed from his own hard-and-fast rules about not getting personally involved in an investigation.

''I've done some work in that area,'' Raine said.

Her reluctance to talk about this was almost palpable. The single sentence was enough, however, to quell Ethan's anxiety. It suggested that she was known to law enforcement because she'd worked with them. Although he was aware that psychics were occasionally used in police work, nobody could be farther from his mental image of that kind of person than Raine.

''More than *some* work,'' Griff corrected. ''During the course of the past ten years, you've been contacted extensively by police departments in many of the major metropolitan areas in the South. Atlanta, Miami, New Orleans,'' Griff listed the names of those cities as he flipped through the pages of the folder in front of him. ''Occasionally by departments as far away as Los Angeles and New York. Many of the officers you worked with speak very highly of your skills, by the way.''

''Thank you.''

"Don't thank me, Ms. McAllister. I'm only repeating what I was told. By more than one person, I might add. They all seemed to feel they'd gotten their money's worth."

Raine said nothing, holding Griff's eyes. Her face was perfectly composed.

"Except you never accepted payment for what you did, did you? Not even in those cases where a reward had been offered."

"I had no use for that money."

"Everyone has a use for money. Especially sculptors, I should think. Or is the notion of the starving artist a myth?"

"Supporting myself has never been a problem."

"At least not since Monty Gardner took you away from your uncle and became your very generous benefactor. Is that right?"

"Mr. Gardner is my father. The words you used to describe what he did have connotations that don't apply in this case."

"Then I apologize for them. Monty Gardner removed you from whatever situation you were in," Griff amended, "and then paid for your education. A very good education, I might add. He even bought the house you live in, didn't he?"

Griff had lifted another page of the file, his eyes scanning the one under it as if seeking information. Ethan knew that was strictly for show. Cabot wouldn't have come to this interview without having memorized every bit of material that had been provided to him concerning Raine McAllister.

"I don't believe Mr. Gardner's financial support of me took anything away from his family. My impression is there was always more than enough money to go around. Unless you believe your wife was in some way deprived because of my relationship with him, I'm not quite sure why you feel you're in a position to question how Mr. Gardner might choose to spend *his* money.''

There was a beat of silence. When Griff spoke again, it was apparent he'd decided to cut his losses and move away from a topic with which he wasn't having a great deal of success.

''Several of the people I talked to in law enforcement indicated that you're no longer available for the kind of services you once provided.''

''That's correct.''

''Is there a reason for that?''

''Of course.''

Griff waited, but Raine refused to fill the strained silence. ''Would you mind telling me what it is?''

''I still do forensic sculpting, but not…the other.''

''Forensic sculpting?''

Griff knew as well as he did what that meant. For some reason he wanted her to put it into words.

''If law enforcement finds a body that can't be identified because of its degree of deterioration, they bring me the skull. I attempt to reconstruct the face.''

''You do that from the bone structure?''

She nodded.

''And from what the bones themselves reveal to you, of course,'' the head of the Phoenix added softly.

It was clear he was no longer inquiring about the process. Griff was commenting on it instead—and as if he knew a great deal about how it was done.

''Sometimes.''

''The people who are most successful at forensic sculpting use intuition as well as a knowledge of physiology. And you have been *remarkably* successful.''

Again Griff waited, and this time, after a small silence, she told him what he obviously wanted to hear.

"Sometimes it's as if I can visualize the person. Almost anyone who does that kind of work will tell you the same thing. It doesn't mean—"

"Remarkably successful at putting flesh on bone," Griff interrupted her explanation as if she hadn't attempted to make it. "Just as you have been far more successful than almost anyone else at finding things that are missing."

"I don't find *things,* Mr. Cabot, as you obviously know. I find people."

There had been something in her voice that made the hair on the back of Ethan's neck lift. Whatever emotion he heard was reflected in her eyes, as well. It wasn't pleasant.

"Particularly children," Griff suggested, his voice as low as hers had been.

"I don't do that anymore."

"Isn't it the same process as remote viewing? Child's play, surely, to someone like you," Griff said, echoing the words she'd used in her description of what she'd done for the CIA.

Raine crossed her arms over her chest, running her left palm along the outside of the opposite arm. "I've told you I can't help you, Mr. Cabot. I can't identify the members of your secret society. I couldn't even guess the intentions of the man who tried to abduct me today."

"But you *did* know what he was capable of," Ethan said, breaking his silence for the first time.

She had told him that the man who pursued her would fire into that crowded cafeteria. And there had been no doubt in her voice when she'd said it.

Her eyes shifted to his face. "That's hardly the same. Everyone has some sense of the inherent good or evil in the people they meet."

"I don't."

"Maybe you call it instinct. Or chemistry."

As she had told Griff, words have certain connotations. To Ethan, her use of that particular one in this situation seemed to imply sexual chemistry.

It made him wonder if she could be aware of his attraction to her. An attraction that had begun almost from the moment she had opened her door to him.

"Is that what you felt about the man at the hospital today?" he asked. "Some…instinct."

"It would be hard to be trusting of anyone who put the muzzle of a 9 mm pistol in your back."

"Especially if you're convinced he'll use it."

There was another, longer silence before she responded. "I thought he would. If he felt he needed to. If he were threatened."

"That's all we're asking you to do for the Phoenix."

With Griff's comment, she turned her attention back to him. "I beg your pardon."

"We'll make the arrangements. All you have to do is mingle with some people we'll introduce you to here in Washington. There'll be a variety of situations—some more intimate than others. Just use your 'instincts.' Then tell Ethan what you think about each person you encounter."

"I've told you—"

"Otherwise he'll need to take you back home in the morning," Cabot interrupted. "You *are* free to make the flight, I take it?"

It took a second for Ethan to realize the last question had been addressed to him. Since his only assignment was the ongoing investigation of The Covenant, he was free to do whatever Griff wanted him to. Even if he didn't like it.

"Of course," he said reluctantly.

"So you see, the decision is entirely up to you, Ms.

McAllister. By the way, if Monty Gardner *is* your father, as you insist, I'm curious as to why you call yourself Mc-Allister?"

"That's what's on my birth certificate. I supposed Mc-Allister was my mother's name."

"And Raine? Rather unusual. Was that her name, too?"

"Actually it's Lorraine. I thought you knew."

"Why would you think that?"

"Because it was his grandmother's name. I was named for her."

The involuntary narrowing of Cabot's eyes, quickly controlled, revealed his surprise. That was one piece of information he *hadn't* known, Ethan realized, despite the thickness of the folder in front of him.

"For Monty's grandmother?"

She nodded. "My father. And I intend to see him again, Mr. Cabot. With or without your approval."

"You claim he sent for you for personal reasons. As far as we're concerned, he gave us your name for strictly professional ones. If you were willing to cooperate with us to that end, however..."

It was blatant blackmail, and they all knew it. Despite Cabot's reputation for being pragmatic, this seemed to Ethan to be taking things to the extreme.

"What about the man who threatened to kill me? Suppose I run into him during one of your *arranged* outings?"

"A very good reason for Ethan's escort while you remain in Washington. I'm sure you'd agree with the logic of that."

"You don't even pretend to believe that I can do what you're asking of me, Mr. Cabot. Neither of you believe it," she said, glancing at Ethan before she turned back to address his superior. "So I don't understand what's behind this proposal."

"I admit to being a skeptic, Ms. McAllister, but as soon as Monty Gardner told us to send for you, someone tried to kill him. And as soon as you arrived today, someone tried to abduct you. I may not believe in your abilities, despite the glowing reports in here." Griff touched the file from which he'd been reading. "I do, however, very much believe in cause and effect. Someone in this town is afraid of you or of what you can tell us. We need to know who that person is, and we need to know why they're afraid."

Raine shook her head. "I'll tell you exactly what I told Ethan last night. I know nothing about The Covenant. Other than what I did for the agency years ago, I have no idea why Mr. Gardner thought I could be useful in your investigation."

"Neither do I. It's enough for me, however, that he did. Do we have a deal? Or does Ethan take you home in the morning?"

"I don't need your permission to see my father. What's to prevent me from walking out of here and going back to the hospital on my own?"

"I should think the memory of that 9 mm pressed against your spine." Griff allowed the threat to rest between them a moment before he went on. "Maybe I'm wrong. Maybe you *aren't* as talented as your devoted fans believe. Or maybe you aren't as clever as *I* think you are."

Their eyes held for endless seconds. They were clearly evaluating one another. Ethan wondered if she could sense the honor and integrity at Griff Cabot's core, despite the unfeeling demand he had just made.

"I repeat, Ms. McAllister," Griff said, choosing to break the stalemate. "The choice is yours."

He closed the folder on his desk. It was an obvious sign of dismissal that anyone associated with the Phoenix would have recognized.

Raine didn't move. Nor did she answer for several long seconds. When she did, surprisingly it was to capitulate to Griff's demands.

"I'll mingle with the people you want me to meet, Mr. Cabot, but be warned. I don't read auras anymore. Or, as evidenced by what happened at the hospital today, not even murderous intent."

"But then, unlike the rest of us, you always have your well-tuned 'instincts' to rely on, don't you?"

Griff's sarcasm was more open than it had been at any other time tonight. Raine's mouth tightened slightly before she rose from her chair.

"You *also* have very good instincts," she said. "When you choose to use them. I'm not sure why you aren't in this case, but you should remember one thing, Mr. Cabot. I'm not the enemy. I may not be the solution you're looking for, but I am also not any part of your problem."

Chapter Seven

Raine couldn't imagine who had chosen the clothes that had been delivered late this afternoon to the hotel suite where she and Ethan had been staying. Griff Cabot seemed far too wed to three-button suits and old school ties to have selected the black lace cocktail dress she was wearing. And the idea that he would have solicited Claire's help in securing a wardrobe for her part in this evening's investigation struck her as ludicrous.

Ethan might have picked out something like this, she acknowledged, making a minor adjustment of the off-the-shoulders neckline. His own clothing indicated that he not only had a sense of style beyond Cabot's expensive buttoned-up elegance, but a feeling for what was most becoming to his tall athlete's body.

For a second the statue of the runner was in her head, the memory so vivid she could feel the clay under her hands, as alive as when she'd been working it. Although she hadn't met Ethan when she'd conceived that sculpture, there was something sensual now in thinking about her fingers molding his body.

As she visualized the figure, she had unconsciously been running her palms over the tightly fitted lace bodice and down to her waist. When she realized what she was doing, she lifted her hands away, holding them out to the side.

A very dangerous combination, she acknowledged. This particular dress and the thought of Ethan Snow.

It had been hard enough during the last forty-eight hours knowing he was in the other bedroom of the suite. She had been all too aware the last two nights that he slept only a few feet away from where she lay tossing and turning, trying to decide if she had done the right thing in giving in to Cabot's blackmail. And trying to decide what role her attraction to Ethan had played in that decision.

She had been determined to see her father again, but she was honest enough, with herself at least, to admit that hadn't been the only consideration. After all, she could have done exactly what she'd threatened to do and returned to the hospital on her own. Aware of the possibility of the kind of attack that had happened yesterday, she wouldn't be so easily caught off guard again.

She had chosen instead to accept Cabot's suggestion that she needed someone to protect her. It hadn't hurt his case that the bodyguard he'd proposed had been the man who had brought her to Washington.

And when she had finally drifted off to sleep last night, her dreams had confirmed what she'd known intuitively from the moment she had opened her door and found Ethan standing on the front deck of the beach house. There was a connection between them that, judging by his resemblance to the statue she'd molded, she'd been aware of even before she'd laid eyes on him.

And tonight…

She denied the thought, substituting a less tantalizing one instead. Tonight she would attend the first of the social events Cabot had arranged. She would spend hours with Ethan as he introduced her to the people the Phoenix wanted her impressions of. Then the two of them would return to this suite....

She shivered involuntarily and discovered that her palms were again flattened over the front of the dress she was wearing, this time slightly below her waist. She glanced up and found her reflection in the mirror.

The fabric of the dress clung to her breasts and hips as if beneath it she were wearing nothing at all. That was obviously the effect the designer had intended since the black lace had been cunningly sewn to a gossamer under-sheath of flesh-colored silk. Surprisingly, the woman in the glass appeared sophisticated enough to carry that illusion off, although the gown was like nothing else she had ever worn.

She had gathered her hair in loose curls at the top of her head. As a concession to the occasion, she had also dark-ened her lashes with mascara, brushed a shimmer of bronzer along her cheekbones and used a tinted gloss on her lips.

She had decided against stockings since her legs were already deeply tanned. The shoes that had been sent with the dress consisted of nothing but a couple of strategically placed black straps attached to three-inch heels.

Obviously not chosen by a woman who has ever had to stand at a cocktail party, she thought, her lips curving into a slight smile.

She took one last look at the finished product and then turned away from the mirror, almost uncomfortable with the image reflected there. As if she were pretending to be someone else. A little girl playing dress-up. Lost in some fantasy world.

If the purpose behind what she had been asked to do tonight for the Phoenix were not so serious, she might have been able to think of the evening in that light. As a role she was playing. Make-believe.

Considering what Ethan believed would happen if they failed to stop The Covenant, however, this was no game. And the investigation had already produced a nearly deadly result.

Despite her doubts about the value of what Cabot proposed she do, she understood that the quicker the Phoenix had answers, the quicker that threat would be removed from her father's life. And from hers.

She had already turned toward the door leading to the central living room of the suite when she remembered there had been something else in the package Ethan had handed her. Although she hadn't been familiar with the name written in gold script across its top, she had recognized the box itself as a jeweler's case.

She had set it aside on the dressing table unopened because she'd never had any great interest in jewelry. Perhaps that was because she'd never owned any, she admitted ruefully, as she picked it up again. At least not anything that had come in a box like this. As she lifted the lid, she vowed that if whatever it contained were too gaudy—

The half-formed thought was destroyed by what she discovered inside. Lying against the black velvet was a pair of earrings.

Far larger than anything she would normally wear, their lozenge shape would dangle perhaps an inch below the lobes of her ears. Despite the fact that, like the dress, she would never have chosen anything remotely like them, there was something about the earrings that drew her.

She put the box down on the dressing table and lifted one of the pair out. As she held it up, the stones caught the light from the chandelier, glittering with an internal fire that left no doubt they were diamonds.

Compelled by their beauty, she lifted the earring to her ear and discovered it was the old-fashioned screw-on kind. From that realization, her absolute certainty they were antiques was instantaneous.

As was her sudden image of another woman. One who had lifted these same jewels to watch them dance and sparkle in the light.

It had been candlelight then that had created their brilliance. And the dress that woman had worn was of a style that hadn't been seen in more than a hundred years.

The vision shimmered away almost as quickly as it had appeared. Raine looked down to find the earring she'd removed from the box was now clutched in her fist.

Slowly she opened her fingers to reveal it shimmering on her palm. She had gripped it so tightly that there were small indentations in her skin on either side of it.

Without any hesitation now, she fastened the earring to the lobe of her ear, making sure it was tight enough to hold securely throughout the evening. Then she lifted the second one from the box and put it on as well. A last look in the mirror assured her that they were the perfect accessory for the dress she wore.

"Thank you, Mr. Cabot," she whispered to her reflection. Then she turned and headed toward the door that would lead to the other part of the suite. And to Ethan Snow.

THE PAST FORTY-EIGHT HOURS had been an exercise in self-control, Ethan admitted. In no way, however, had they prepared him for the sight of Raine standing in the doorway to her bedroom, dressed to attend one of the most prestigious events of the Washington season.

He'd seen her half a dozen times since they'd checked in to the suite two nights ago. Necessary encounters, since he'd been the one who had ordered and accepted their meals from room service, answered the phone and inspected the packages that had arrived this afternoon. All those meetings had left him looking forward to the next opportunity to interact with her.

The last had come less than three hours ago. Cabot had kept his promise to keep Raine informed about Montgomery Gardner's condition. Thankfully the news today had been much better. The old man had not yet fully regained consciousness, but there had been encouraging improvements in his responses to outside stimuli.

When Ethan had knocked on her door to relay that news, Raine had been wearing a pair of jeans and a knit top, her face devoid of makeup. And she'd again been barefoot, just as at the beach house.

The transformation she'd undergone between then and now couldn't have been more complete. Or more startling.

His body responded, his groin hardening instantly. As if he were sixteen instead of thirty-six.

The black lace dress was cut straight across the shoulders, revealing a tan that clearly hadn't come from any bottle. Her hair had been put up, perhaps to better display the only jewelry she wore—a pair of diamond earrings that caught the light whenever she moved her head. High-heeled black sandals and a small evening bag completed the ensemble.

"I'm ready when you are," she said.

Her eyes then made the same slow assessment of his appearance that he had just made of hers. He wondered if his had been as obvious. Or as unnerving.

Unable to return to his apartment because that would leave Raine unprotected, Ethan had asked fellow Phoenix agent John Edmonds to pick up the things he thought he'd need during the next few days. Given tonight's assignment, the tuxedo he was wearing had been one of them.

He'd showered and shaved, of course, but he had changed into the familiar clothing quickly, hardly glancing into the mirror until he'd had to tie the black tie. Now, for the first time in years, he found himself wondering what a woman thought about his appearance.

"You look…" he began, and then hesitated. There seemed no reason not to state the obvious, however. "Amazing," he finished softly.

For a moment it seemed as if she were evaluating the word to determine if he had intended it to be mocking. With the obvious admiration in his eyes, her mouth finally relaxed, the corners tilting.

"Thank you. Think we'll manage not to embarrass Mr. Cabot?"

Griff had acquired the tickets to tonight's dinner, the only fund-raising event openly sponsored by The Covenant, several weeks ago. The Phoenix had already planned to have a presence there tonight, even if they were still working in the dark. The event had been part of the reason they'd decided to contact Montgomery Gardner to see if he could possibly add anything to what little they knew about the clandestine organization.

Now that Raine was working with them, the dinner was the perfect opportunity for her to make some initial assessments. Most of the people who had ended up on Ethan's list of possible members of The Covenant would also be in attendance. As would almost everyone else who had enough money to make them interesting to charities, he conceded.

Now that he'd read the file the Phoenix agents had put together on the woman standing before him, Ethan was less skeptical than he had been about how valuable her intuition might prove to be. Comments from law enforcement officers all over the country, men who were no more given to buying into sideshow scams than he was, had made an impression. He wasn't yet ready to embrace the old CIA premise of using psychics in intel, but what Raine had been able to accomplish in some of the criminal cases he'd read about had been powerfully convincing.

Griff had dismissed his comment about those with the reminder that cops searching for clues in a case that has stymied them *want* to believe someone can help—especially if those cases involve the life of a child. And wanting to believe that much went more than halfway to meeting the burden of proof.

Griff had no faith in Raine's ability to separate the good guys from the bad. His motives in sending them to this dinner tonight had more to do with the hope, or maybe with the expectation, that she would provoke the same kind of response her presence at the hospital had.

Ethan was bothered by the thought that Griff was using Raine as bait, but he was also determined not to let anything happen to her. With the very real threat of an epidemic of homegrown terrorism hanging over their heads, perhaps this was one case where the end would justify the means. Even these.

"Will he be there?" she asked.

Lost in those thoughts, it took him a second to realize who she meant. "Griff?"

"And Claire."

"I don't know," Ethan confessed.

If Griff planned to attend the dinner, he hadn't let Ethan in on his intentions. Even if he did, Ethan doubted that his wife would accompany him. Not with her grandfather still in such serious condition.

Claire's globe-trotting parents had just returned this afternoon from Russia, where they'd been vacationing when they'd received the news. Of course, he didn't feel that he was at liberty to share that information with someone outside the family.

And that, too, he remembered, was still open to question. Griff had uncovered nothing that indicated Montgomery Gardner had ever acknowledged Raine as his daughter. And despite Griff's contacts within the agency, he'd been unable to secure any records pertaining to Raine. Even after enlisting assistant deputy director Carl Steiner's help, they'd been unable to get any information on the Cassandra Project, the experiment she claimed to have worked on.

"Then I suppose we're on our own," Raine said.

Ethan thought he detected a trace of relief in that pronouncement. Since he'd felt a growing anxiety during most of the afternoon, he was surprised she seemed so calm about the evening that lay ahead. Maybe that was a good sign.

If you believe in signs…

"Shall we?" he said, opening the outer door.

She walked across the room, meeting his eyes before she stepped through it and into the hall. The upward glance through her lashes had been brief, but the impact was enough to leave his mouth dry.

Hand trembling slightly, he pulled the door to the suite closed behind them, following her to the elevator. The height of the heels she wore caused a slight sway to her hips as she walked, which produced the same aching hardness as his first sight of her in that dress had.

Griff was hoping to provoke a reaction from the leaders of The Covenant to Raine's appearance at their dinner tonight. Whatever that reaction was, Ethan acknowledged, it probably wasn't going to be the same one she would have on the majority of the men she encountered.

Chapter Eight

It had been so long since Raine had deliberately tried to open her consciousness to the emotions that surrounded her that it was as if she had forgotten how. At first there had been almost nothing. And then, despite her own skepticism, she had begun to sense the feelings of the people around her.

Perhaps her deep resentment of Cabot's mockery played a role in her success. Or the desire to prove to Ethan that he was wrong to doubt her. Or her growing self-confidence that the gift she had denied so long wasn't entirely lost.

Gradually a cacophony of impressions assaulted her, few of which were clear or meaningful. And none of which seemed threatening.

She wasn't sure how much Ethan was aware of what she was experiencing, but as they had made their way across the lobby to the crowded elevator bank and then up to the hotel's famous rooftop ballroom, she could feel his support surrounding her like an aura. After being alone as long as she had, there was something incredibly appealing about someone being concerned for what she was feeling.

The predinner cocktail hour had been relatively un-eventful, at least from the perspective of what she'd been asked to do. No one she'd been introduced to had set off alarm bells. Of course if, as Cabot believed, someone really were afraid of her abilities, they would probably take pains to avoid just this kind of situation.

The group of ten seated with them at the round table where they'd found their place cards had been friendly and readily engaged them in conversation. One couple seemed to know Ethan, at least socially. Raine was aware of an undercurrent of interest on their part about the woman he was escorting tonight. None of their questions—the standard ones about where she and Ethan had met and how long they'd been dating—had been particularly pointed, but couched within them was an obvious curiosity about their relationship.

Ethan had handled the inquiries smoothly by telling them that he'd gone to school with her brother. The explanation sounded perfectly credible and seemed to be accepted.

Actually, he was very good at lying, Raine decided, listening to his story. Most people who weren't telling the truth went out of their way to convince their listeners they were. Ethan provided just enough information to satisfy the questions he'd been asked, but not enough to be suspicious.

Maybe the CIA trained their operatives in that skill. Or maybe Cabot had done that. He, too, knew the value of not saying too much.

As the celebrity spokesperson for the charity took his place at the podium, the lights in the ballroom dimmed. In conjunction with a PowerPoint presentation, the toastmaster began a prolonged recital of the year's successes, allowing Raine to turn her undivided attention to the task she'd agreed to perform.

She focused first on the guests seated nearby, willing herself to relax and receive whatever impressions came to her. She had learned long ago that she couldn't force any of this.

She soon realized it wouldn't take a clairvoyant to know that most of the crowd was politely bored. As she considered faces in the dark anonymity of the ballroom, sometimes a flare of anger or anxiety emanating from someone would disrupt her concentration.

She had to fight a tendency to linger over any kind of negative emotion, even petty ones, trying to fit them into the scenario she thought Cabot was interested in. So far, however, she'd felt nothing that suggested the degree of hatred or fanaticism necessary for any act of terrorism.

She was focusing on the third table when a sensation like a cold finger ran down her spine. That precognition was followed by a searing flood of malevolence. The feeling was surprisingly powerful, enough so that she had automatically closed her mind against its force before she realized this might be exactly what Cabot had sent her to uncover.

She hurriedly examined the faces of the people at her own table, searching for any indication that what she'd just felt had come from one of them. As intense as the sensation was, she believed it must have originated from someone in very close proximity.

Most of her tablemates, however, appeared to be focused on the speaker. She could pick up no residual hostility at all. And whatever she had sensed only seconds ago seemed to have disappeared.

"What's wrong?"

Ethan had bent toward her to whisper the question against her ear. To anyone observing them, the posture he'd assumed would look like a lover taking the opportunity the darkness provided to whisper some endearment or to brush his lips against her temple. In their case, of course…

She leaned back, widening the distance between them so

that she could look into his eyes. Their normal slate gray appeared almost black in the dimness.

Again an awareness of his solicitude washed over her in a wave, almost obliterating the memory of the animosity she'd just felt. She shook her head, trying to think how to describe what had occurred.

"I don't know. Something... Something very strange just happened. An incredibly strong feeling of malice—"

She was aware that the feminine half of the couple who'd claimed a prior acquaintance with Ethan was watching them. Raine smiled at her, receiving a quick, commiserating grin in return.

When the woman had returned her attention to the speaker, Ethan whispered, "From her?"

Raine shook her head again. She was still unsure where that sense of enmity had originated, but she had already decided it hadn't been with any of the people at their table.

Other than that, all she could be certain of was its power. And that it had been directed at her.

During her work with the law enforcement community, she had come in contact with genuine evil on several occasions. What she had sensed then had been a generalized hatred, directed at the world at large and all who walked upon it. This, in contrast, had been personal. And for some reason she felt that the hatred had been deliberately revealed.

An attempt to frighten her? If so, whoever had exposed so much of their intent would probably be pleased with the result.

Before she'd arrived in Washington, it had been more than three years since she had felt any sense of threat. She didn't like it any better now than she had then.

Even as that thought formed, Ethan picked up her hand, which had been resting on the table beside her plate, and placed it between the two of his. When she felt the warm strength of his callused palm under hers, she realized how cold her fingers had grown. And, embarrassingly, how much they were trembling.

''Then who?'' Ethan was near enough that she could feel his breath against her cheek. The question had been soft but demanding.

Again the woman across the table glanced in their direction. Noticing Raine's eyes on her, she quickly looked back at the speaker.

''I don't know,'' Raine said. ''I couldn't tell. Somewhere close. From behind us, maybe?''

She wasn't sure where that impression had come from. It hadn't been in her head only seconds before, but it was now.

Ethan turned his head, his lips nuzzling her temple as he considered the tables she'd indicated. Searching for someone who had made his list of suspected Covenant members?

Whatever he was doing, he was so close she could smell the soap he'd used in his shower tonight. Or maybe it was his aftershave. Something entirely masculine, in either case. Sandalwood with a hint of musk.

At one time that fragrance had been considered an aphrodisiac. With Ethan's chest brushing her shoulder as he studied the tables behind them, for the first time she understood why.

''Are you all right?'' he whispered.

She wanted to say no. She wanted to tell him to get her out of there. Not just physically out of the room, but out of a situation that could generate the kind of malice she had felt.

She nodded instead, trying to control both her fear and any outward sign of her reaction to his nearness. His thumb moved from side to side across the back of her hand, a gesture she knew was intended to be comforting.

It was also highly provocative. Especially as emotionally vulnerable as she was right now. She wondered if he understood what he was doing to her, and then answered her own question.

A man like this doesn't reach maturity without being well aware of the effect he has on women.

Besides, as he held her hand, two of his fingers rested under the pulse in her wrist. He would be able to feel her increased heart rate. Whether he would attribute its rapidity to the sensation she'd described or to his nearness was another question.

"I'm all right. It was just…unnerving."

True enough. And the admission would serve to mask the fact that his touch also unnerved her.

"Threatening?"

"I thought so."

"And you're sure you have no idea—"

Before he could repeat the question, she began to shake her head. Apparently Ethan moved at the same time. His cheek grazed hers, its slight masculine abrasiveness as sensual as the movement of his thumb across her knuckles had been.

The combination of threat and sexual awareness was something she'd never experienced before. She couldn't deny that she found it exciting—the idea that this man, to whom she was already so strongly attracted, had been charged with protecting her from whoever had sent those negative thoughts.

"Anyone back there on your list?" she managed, despite the growing clamor in her lower body.

He straightened, increasing the distance between them. Raine realized only then that the speaker was finishing up.

She eased a breath, grateful she'd been given an opportunity to regain control before the lights came up. Ethan Snow was proving to be a far greater distraction than she had ever imagined any man could be for her.

"Several," he whispered. "When the lights come up, look around and see if you can tell where that sensation originated."

The fact that he had apparently accepted what she'd told him was a small victory, but it was one she savored. The lights brightened as the guests began to applaud the presentation. Raine shifted in her seat, pushing her evening bag off her lap as she did.

She intended to use the opportunity to pick it up as an excuse to look at the table behind her. Before she could reach for the purse, the man seated on her right had retrieved it, holding it out to her with a smile.

"Thank you," she said, managing only a quick glance over her shoulder.

No one at the next table was paying the slightest attention to her. There was the normal whispering and gathering up of belongings as the master of ceremonies continued to thank those responsible for the success of the evening. His final announcement was that the pledge cards would be collected from each table.

The evening was over, except for the same kind of casual mingling that had preceded the meal. And she was no closer to identifying any of the people the Phoenix was interested in than she had been at its beginning.

"Have we met? Before tonight, I mean?"

The question posed by the man who'd retrieved her purse caused her to turn her attention from the table behind her and back to him. His sun-streaked hair was a little longer than would normally appeal to her. However, deeply tanned and possessing a pair of smiling blue eyes, he was handsome in a California beach boy kind of way.

She tried to think of the name by which he'd introduced himself as they'd been finding their places. Brian or Brett. Something with a B, but that was all she could remember.

"I don't think so," she said.

"You *could* have softened that blow by saying you'd surely have remembered if we had," he suggested, smiling at her.

He was flirting, she realized belatedly. And doing it rather openly, considering that Ethan was on her other side. Of course, Ethan was occupied right now with the woman across the table, the one who'd been curious about their relationship and then so interested in their conversation.

"I'm sure I would have," she said.

She was aware that Ethan was in the process of getting to his feet, although he was still talking to the other couple. She prepared for him to pull out her chair, but the stranger on her right stood instead and put his hand on the back of it.

"May I?"

Unable to refuse without seeming rude, Raine allowed him to help her up. "Thank you."

"Brad Davis. Just in case you didn't remember that, either."

"Thank you, Mr. Davis."

"Brad. I'm certain we've met before. The museum party perhaps?"

"I don't think so," Raine said, this time deliberately turning away from him.

She put her hand on Ethan's arm, causing him to look down at her questioningly. She smiled at him and then, still smiling, pretended to listen as he disengaged himself from the couple who seemed determined to arrange a future meeting. He did it as skillfully as he had fielded their earlier questions about his relationship with Raine.

"Ready?" he asked finally.

"I thought there was someone you wanted me to meet," she suggested.

His eyes narrowed slightly, but he didn't argue. He turned and started toward the table behind them. Raine maintained her hold on his arm, feeling her apprehension grow with each step, despite the fact that this had been her idea.

"Ethan."

The man who spoke was in his early fifties, perhaps, and several inches shorter than Ethan's six-two. He wore a badly fitting tux and seemed to be alone. His dark eyes darted to her face before they returned to Ethan's.

"Carl," he said with a quick nod to the man who'd approached them.

"And this must be Ms. McAllister."

"Raine, this is Carl Steiner."

"I've heard a great deal about you," Steiner said, offering his hand. Whoever had taught him etiquette had obviously neglected the niceties.

"Really?" she said, softening the question with a smile.

"We have mutual friends."

It was the same thing Ethan had said when she'd tried to close the door in his face. He had been talking about her father. She wondered if Steiner might also know Monty Gardner, and if so, in what capacity.

Because he was still rather pointedly holding out his hand, she finally put hers into his. And then wished that she hadn't.

There was something about the man that made her flesh crawl. It wasn't the feeling of threat she'd experienced a few minutes ago. It was more the way someone looks at you when they believe they have you at a disadvantage. As if they know something unsavory about you, some unpleasant secret you'd hoped no one would ever know.

"And who would that be?" she asked, removing her fingers from his as quickly as she could.

His thin lips moved upward at the corners, but like the man at the hospital, the smile never reached his eyes. She wouldn't have believed it if it had.

Steiner ignored her question, turning to say something to Ethan instead. Although he was almost whispering, she caught the name Griff.

Hearing that allowed her to relax a little. Steiner obviously had some connection to the CIA. What she had believed to be a reference to her father and now his use of Cabot's first name made that obvious.

"Have you two met Representative Crosston?" Steiner asked.

He put his hand on Ethan's elbow, urging him toward a small knot of people nearby. Raine had obviously been included in the invitation, but she was unwilling to spend another moment in Steiner's company. She felt soiled by the brief contact she'd had with him.

As Ethan walked over to shake hands with the congressman, she allowed her eyes to survey the others at Steiner's table. As she scanned each face, she found no echo of the enmity she'd felt before.

There was nothing here to set off alarms. Only people who were anxious now to leave. Eager to beat the traffic. To get home and send their baby-sitters on their way. To take off their shoes and their evening wear and climb into bed and sleep late tomorrow.

She had been wrong in thinking that someone at this table had been the source of that malice. What she did had never been an exact science, and with the aftermath of what had happened three years ago, it was apparently far less so now.

Even as she made that acknowledgment, the sensation came again, almost as powerful as before. Only not as close, she realized. Not down here at all, but—

Her eyes lifted, searching the balcony above the ballroom floor where the tables for the gala had been set up. Suddenly there was no doubt in her mind of exactly where that feeling had emanated.

Someone was standing in the shadows at the top of the staircase that led up to the mezzanine. Hidden from view, he was watching her.

A sense of threat, as direct as the beam of a flashlight, sliced through her consciousness. She turned, searching for Ethan. Steiner, his hand on Ethan's shoulder, had pulled him into another group of people and was busy making introductions.

''Ethan?''

Her voice seemed to echo inside her head, so that she wasn't sure she had said his name aloud. Ethan didn't respond, so perhaps she hadn't.

Steiner was still talking, his hand rising and falling as he patted the taller man's shoulder. It seemed to be moving in slow motion. Just as the noises around her were fading. Becoming only a background for the important thing that was happening.

Her eyes flicked back to the shadows on the balcony. The force of what she felt hadn't lessened. If anything, it seemed to have intensified, becoming more and more compelling. She shook her head, trying to clear it. Nothing changed.

Then, without making any conscious decision to do so,

she took a single step forward. And then another. And another. As she continued to move toward it, her eyes were fastened intently on that pool of darkness at the top of the stairs.

Chapter Nine

One minute Raine had been there, her hand on his arm, and the next she was gone. Steiner's insistence on introducing him to someone had momentarily sidetracked him, but Ethan would have sworn he hadn't been distracted for more than a minute.

Long enough, he thought bitterly.

Despite the advantage his height gave him, he couldn't spot Raine in the sea of people beginning to eddy toward the exits. She couldn't have gone far, he told himself, trying to quell his rising sense of panic.

It seemed only a matter of seconds that he hadn't been aware of her by his side. Just as he'd been acutely aware of her all night.

"Something wrong?" As usual, Steiner's eyes were devoid of expression, but his voice held a note of what sounded like genuine concern.

"Ms. McAllister. She was here a moment ago, and now she's disappeared."

As Ethan continued to scan the crowd, conscious of seconds ticking away, his anxiety grew. He had seen no need to prevaricate with Steiner. Maybe while Ethan had been exchanging social niceties with the assistant deputy director's guests, Steiner had been keeping an eye on Raine.

After all, his interest in her when they'd been introduced had been quite open.

Steiner's gaze focused briefly on the people making their way toward the central doors of the ballroom, which led to the bank of elevators, before it came back to Ethan. "Maybe she went to the ladies' room."

It was a possibility. Considering what had happened at the hospital, Ethan would have thought Raine understood the necessity of staying close to him tonight. Griff had certainly been explicit about the dangers she faced.

"You know where that would be?" Ethan surveyed the room, looking for the typical discreet sign and directional arrow.

His gaze swept hurriedly across the staircase on the other side of the room, its elaborate wrought iron banisters leading up to the balcony that ran around the top of the ballroom. His attention snapped back to it almost immediately.

His mind's eye had belatedly registered a figure at the top of those steps. By the time his attention had returned to the stairs, whoever he'd seen there had already disappeared into the shadows of the balcony.

Raine?

He examined that fleeting impression. The figure had definitely been that of a woman. And she'd been wearing a dark dress. Black? It might have been, but the glimpse he'd gotten had been so fleeting…

He had already taken a step toward the staircase when Steiner's hand fastened around his forearm. "I think the rest rooms are over there." The CIA's assistant deputy director pointed to a location in the opposite direction of where Ethan had been headed.

There was no reason for Raine to have been climbing up to that balcony alone, Ethan acknowledged. And no one could have forcibly abducted her in the midst of this crowd.

Not even by employing the same tactics the man at the hospital had used. All she would have had to do was to call his name.

A far more logical explanation for her disappearance was the one Steiner had suggested. Maybe Raine had decided to slip away to the rest room while he'd been engaged with the congressman Carl had insisted he meet. He looked toward the sign Steiner had indicated and then back toward the stairs.

Maybe you call it instinct.

He didn't. He had always called it going with his gut. And that was exactly what he intended to do this time.

"Thanks," he said to Steiner. Without a backward glance, he headed in the direction opposite to the one the CIA supervisor had pointed out.

WHEN RAINE REACHED the top of the stairs, the shadowed area she'd noticed from below was empty. Actually, the entire balcony appeared to be deserted. Given the number of people who had crowded into the ballroom tonight that seemed strange.

And it made coming here a very foolish move on her part, she admitted.

She couldn't explain why she'd decided to strike out on her own. The entire point of having Ethan escort her was to preclude what had occurred at the hospital from happening again.

Besides, now that she was here, the compulsion that had draw her up the stairs seemed to have faded. She couldn't imagine why she'd thought identifying the source of that animosity was so urgent that she couldn't wait for Ethan to accompany her.

She stepped over to the railing to look down on the crowd below, searching for him. She couldn't find his tall, tuxedo-clad body in the swirling mass of people, although she did spot Steiner. He was still conversing with the people he'd been so insistent Ethan should meet, but there was no sign of the Phoenix operative in the group surrounding him.

Maybe Ethan was looking for her. After all, according to Cabot his assignment tonight had been to keep an eye on her.

By coming up here while he'd been engaged, she had made that virtually impossible. She couldn't understand why she had done that, especially when that impulse had been in response to what could only be called a strong sense of hostility.

Despite how foolish this had been, no harm had been done, she decided, turning to head back to the stairs. Before she had taken more than a couple of steps, the sensation she'd felt on the floor of the ballroom returned with a vengeance.

Far more powerful than it had been before, it was obviously much closer. Or maybe more focused.

Despite the same inexplicable urge to find its source, she started forward again, her eyes once more searching the crowd below. This time, with an enormous sense of relief, she spotted Ethan.

He was pushing his way through the throng with a single-minded determination. And thankfully he was headed in the direction of the staircase.

At that moment he raised his eyes, seeming to look right into hers. Raine wondered if he could see her, since she was in the darkest area of the balcony. Actually, she was standing almost in the exact spot from which the animosity she'd felt downstairs had seemed to originate.

As she stared down at Ethan, something brushed her arm. She whirled, reacting to the unexpected contact.

In the deepest part of the shadows behind her stood a figure from a nightmare, draped from head to foot in black. He was wearing a cloak, she realized, her eyes straining through the dimness, trying desperately to make sense out of what she was seeing. A cloak *and* a mask, the kind that covered the entire face.

All but the eyes. They were visible through the slits in the dark material from which the mask had been fashioned.

As she met them, the same flashbulb transformation that had happened in her studio occurred again.

The now-familiar image of the pond, its waters still and deep and cold, replaced the eyes peering through the holes in the mask. Eyes that in the brief moment she looked into them had perfectly reflected those same chilling characteristics.

WHATEVER ETHAN THOUGHT he'd seen at the top of the staircase had no longer been there when he'd arrived. Instead, it appeared there was no one at all on the entire balcony. He had walked its perimeter twice, stopping several times to study the scene below with an anxiety that was fast becoming desperation.

There was still no sign of Raine, and by now the crowd was beginning to thin. Where the hell could she have gone?

He found it hard to believe that he'd allowed himself to be distracted like that. Maybe it was because they'd been in such close contact seconds before she'd disappeared. Or maybe his failure to anticipate that anything could happen to her was because the group surrounding them had all been Steiner's associates or members of the Intelligence Committee.

And maybe if you try a little harder, you can latch on to some other excuse for an action that was inexcusable.

He started back toward the stairs, intending to take

Steiner's advice and check out the ladies' room. They were always more crowded at an event like this. Maybe Raine was standing in a line, worrying about not having told him where she was heading.

No matter what scenarios he invented, he was fairly certain that a trip to the powder room couldn't explain her prolonged absence. He couldn't call Griff and report her missing, however, without checking out every possibility. A phone call he would give anything not to have to make.

As he approached the area near the top of the stairs, he realized the reason it was so much darker than the rest of the balcony. The bulb in one of the art deco electric wall sconces had burned out.

Passing through the shadows created by its loss, he glanced over the wrought iron railing one last time, his gaze sweeping across the remaining guests. Searching for dark hair, loosely gathered into curls. For a head carried regally on a long elegant neck. For smooth, slim shoulders framed by black lace.

Disappointed with the results of his search, he directed his eyes back to the stairs he was about to descend. Just at the top of them something glittered against the deep maroon of the old-fashioned patterned carpet.

Even before he had stooped to pick it up, he identified the object. It was one of the pair of earrings Raine had been wearing tonight, highly distinctive because, even to his relatively untrained eye, they had appeared to be antique and valuable.

They were also the kind that screwed onto the ear, a method that was supposed to provide security against loss. So what had happened on this spot to dislodge this one?

His hand reflexively clenched the earring as his eyes examined the area where it had been lying. There was no other information to be gleaned from the smooth surface of the carpeting. Even if some kind of struggle had taken place on this spot, the hard nap wouldn't have been marked.

At least he had proof now that his instinct had been correct. Raine *had* been here, and only a little while ago. Since he was sure she hadn't gone down those stairs in the few minutes it had taken him to get to them, that must mean—

There had to be another access to this area. Bolstered by the certainty that he was now on the right track, he began to retrace the journey he'd made along the balcony, looking for another exit.

This time he found what he had missed before. Covered by a gold brocade curtain was a set of double doors that matched those in the ballroom below.

He pressed the latch of the handle with his thumb, but it didn't give. Locked. Which didn't necessarily mean that they had been minutes ago.

He bent, examining the mechanism. Considering the age of the hotel, what he found was exactly what he'd expected.

He straightened, hurriedly taking his billfold out of his inside coat pocket to remove a credit card. He inserted the thin plastic between the doors, pushing the tongue of the lock toward the back. It slid out of the notch in the opposite door, just as he'd expected.

Wherever these led, the management hadn't been worried enough about anyone making an unauthorized entrance through them to change the locks to something more modern and more secure. He wasn't sure whether that was comforting or not.

Especially since he had no weapon. Security at social functions in the capital right now was too tight to allow that, even for someone licensed to carry.

He took a deep breath, then pushed the door inward. And knew immediately why this exit hadn't been more secured. The doors opened onto an exterior hallway that matched almost exactly the configuration of the interior balcony that overlooked the ballroom, except here, instead of a railing, there were windows set at regular intervals along what must be the outside wall of the hotel.

He couldn't guess at the original purpose in splitting the space in this way, but it was obvious that through the years, the exterior part of the balcony had become a storage area for items that might be needed in the ballroom below. Gold and white chairs, like the ones that had surrounded the tables at dinner tonight were stacked on top of one another. There were also stacks of extra tables and what appeared to be some kind of lighting equipment. That was probably set up on the balcony itself and could be directed onto the dance floor. There were even racks of what appeared to be costumes. Maybe used by the wait staff for holiday parties or other special occasions?

He stepped through the doorway and into the outer corridor, which was uncarpeted. With nothing to absorb it, sound would carry along its entire length.

He eased the door closed behind him and then stood a few seconds in the resulting darkness. He could hear nothing but his own breathing.

He resisted the urge to call Raine's name. Just because he couldn't hear anything didn't mean there was no one else here.

His eyes finally adjusted to the loss of light that had resulted from closing the balcony door. The long windows along the outer wall were uncovered and, despite the darkness outside, provided some illumination. Enough to allow him to navigate around the obstacles the open door had revealed, now little more than shapes in the darkness.

Having seen this area, which was more like a warehouse than a part of the elegant ballroom below, he didn't believe Raine would have come in here alone.

Wild-goose chase.

Only the earring he had slipped into his pocket kept him from giving in to those doubts and retracing his steps to place that call to Griff. There was no logical reason for Raine to be up here wandering around among the stage props.

Not unless she'd been brought in here.

He began to move forward. No matter how careful he tried to be, the soles of his shoes made noise on the concrete floor, which echoed and reechoed in the narrow space.

So much for any element of surprise.

Choosing speed rather than caution, he began to walk without regard for the sounds of his footsteps. Once around the circle, he promised himself, and if he didn't find anything, he'd go back downstairs. He couldn't put off calling Griff any longer.

He had made perhaps half the circle when he realized there was some subliminal sound besides the noise he was making. Originating from somewhere ahead of him, there was a tantalizing familiarity about it. Something he knew he should be able to identify…

And when he had, he also knew why he was hearing it only now. One of the windows on the outside wall was open. Carried on the night air, the sound of traffic on the street below was drifting upward and into the corridor.

He rounded the curve, and the open window was visible. The noises were louder here, mostly the swish of tires as a vehicle passed on the damp streets below and the occasional bleat of a distant horn.

Maybe the hotel staff used the open window for ventilation, his rational mind suggested. Seeing it, however, whatever instinct had carried him this far tightened his stomach and sent the same icy finger he'd felt in Griff's office racing down his spine. Something was terribly wrong about that open window.

Having reached that decision, he quickened his pace. Although there was more light here because there was no grimed glass between the corridor and the sky, in his rush he stumbled over something.

Off balance, he staggered forward, careening into the wall before he could right himself. With a grunt of pain at the force of his landing, he turned, trying to see what had tripped him.

In the moonlight a spill of black lay against the paler gray of the concrete floor. For a fraction of a second, Ethan thought it might be blood.

But of course, whatever had caught the toe of his shoe and sent him staggering hadn't been liquid. It had been something solid. Something tangible.

Fabric? Black fabric?

Using the hand he'd flattened against the wall to break his fall, he pushed away from it, literally forcing himself to take the few steps that would bring him back to that pool of black.

He bent, fingers reaching forward. Without making contact, they hesitated in midair, reluctant to touch the object on the dusty floor. Stomach churning, he had to force his hand to close over it.

When it did, he realized it was cloth, just as he'd feared. He started to lift it and knew, even before he had held it up to the dim outside light, that it wasn't what he had feared it might be.

The fabric was smooth under his fingers. Not lace, he acknowledged, closing his eyes in relief as he finally remembered to take a breath.

No lingering scent of the woman who had worn that

sophisticated black dress clung to the material he held. Whatever this was smelled slightly of mildew.

He had a strong inclination to drop it. To leave it lying where he'd found it. Instead, acting on the instinct that had guided him this far, he held it up before the moonlit window.

At first it seemed shapeless, nothing more than a piece of cloth. Suddenly, with a chill of understanding, he realized what he held.

A long, black cape with an attached collar. And there was a drawstring by which it could be fastened around the wearer's neck.

Once he'd determined the basic structure of the garment, Ethan turned it so that he held it up by the shoulders, which were heavily padded. To disguise the size or shape of whoever put it on?

One of the costumes off the rack? Or a prop? Whatever it was, he decided, it had nothing to do with Råine. Or with her disappearance.

He turned, carelessly tossing the garment over the sill of the open window as he leaned through it to peer at the scene below. Streetlights marched in perfect order toward the Potomac. Despite the hour, traffic was fairly heavy, its familiar sounds clear in the still night air.

Both hands on the sill, he had already begun to push his body back out of the window when out of the corner of his eye, he caught a glimpse of something that shouldn't be there.

Each of the windows had a small outside balcony, which extended no more than a foot or perhaps eighteen inches from the wall. It was surrounded by concrete balustrades topped by a flat rail of the same material. Hardly wide enough for a man to stand on comfortably, the space was obviously intended for decorative purposes only.

Between the pseudo-balcony of the window he was leaning out and the next was a gradually curving ledge, perhaps half the width of the space that was included in each narrow enclosure. And on the ledge to his right was a shape.

He tried to tell himself that what he was seeing was part of the architecture. A statue or ornamentation.

In an attempt to verify that, he glanced to his left and found only smooth wall stretching above the curving ledge. Slowly he turned back to his right.

With a thrill of horror, he realized that what he was seeing was *not* a part of the building. It was instead the woman who had been the object of his search. And she was standing on a ledge no wider than his foot, more than a hundred feet above the ground.

Chapter Ten

She first became aware of the humid night air against her face. And then the sound of traffic far below. She hadn't dared look down, afraid of what she might see. Instead, she had pressed her body against the wall behind her, knowing instinctively that it represented safety.

She had realized almost instantly where she was. Not the location, of course, but the situation. And she found she had no idea how she'd gotten here.

Like the unexplained passage of time when she'd seen the vision of the pond, there seemed to be a gap in her memory. The last thing she remembered was standing in the ballroom, looking at the stairs that led to the balcony.

She closed her eyes, but somehow the interior darkness was worse than the other. She opened them again to look out on the panorama of the night sky spread out before her.

Had she had another vision? Or was there a different explanation for this missing time? Whatever its cause, she had apparently been brought or forced outside, to a place high above the traffic in the streets, whose sounds she could hear below.

Keeping the base of her spine against the wall, she slowly moved her hands, sliding her palms over the rough-textured stonework behind her until she felt her position was as stable as she could make it. Then, by careful degrees, she lowered her head until she was looking down.

She'd paid no attention to the number Ethan had punched on the elevator they'd taken to the ballroom. The taillights of the cars below were small enough, however, that she knew she must be at least a dozen stories up.

Without moving her head, she cut her eyes to the right. In her peripheral vision she could see the wall she was leaning against curving away from her. Along it ran the narrow ledge she was apparently standing on, and it was no wider than the length of her foot.

Frightened by the reality of her situation, she raised her chin too quickly, bumping her head against the wall behind her. Immediately she overcompensated for that error by leaning forward. As she did, her right hand came away from the wall.

Feeling as if she were on the verge of losing her balance, she spread her fingers like talons, trying to get a grip on the stone. When she had, she closed her eyes again, forcing herself to concentrate on taking the next breath. Breathe in. And out. In and out.

The deep inhalations didn't ease her sense of panic. All they did was make her light-headed.

She closed her mouth, trying to focus on anything but where she was. Her mind seized on the mystery of who had forced her out here and why. Had he intended her to fall? Had he arranged this so that her death would appear to be a suicide or an accident?

If so, this seemed a ridiculously convoluted way to go about it. Why not shove her under a bus? Or pay someone to run her down in the street? Why arrange this kind of elaborate charade?

Suddenly there was some noise to her left. She fought the instinct to turn her head too quickly, having learned what the slightest miscalculation might lead to. Instead, she held her breath, listening for whatever she'd heard to be repeated.

Was the person who had forced her onto this ledge still there? Was he planning to startle her in an attempt to make her fall? Could anyone be that diabolical?

But of course they could. This was no game. She had felt the strength of their hatred. And it had been personal. Very personal.

Someone she knew? Someone who knew her? From the first time she had been in Washington all those years ago?

Or was this her father's enemy, seeking to hurt him by hurting her. After all, someone had already attacked him. Maybe since they had failed at that—

Again she heard the unidentified noise on her left. Was he waiting there, watching her, like some fat, evil spider?

The analogy worked on so many levels that she forced herself to concentrate on it. Something to think about other than what he might be doing.

She had been caught in his web. Like some foolish moth attracted to a flame, she had been drawn to him by the hostility he'd deliberately projected. Her action in leaving the ballroom to seek him out was something she could neither explain nor justify. She had put herself into the hands of the enemy, and now he was toying with her.

Another noise, this one more subtle. Nothing but a brush of movement against the stones. Was he inching his way along the ledge toward her?

If so, there would be nothing she could do to resist. No movement that would not send her plunging to the ground below.

"Raine."

Instantly she knew the voice that had spoken her name. And she almost responded to it. Almost turned toward the sound. Just in time she resisted the impulse, leaning back against the wall behind her as her knees went weak with relief.

"Ethan?" She breathed his name, hardly daring to move her lips.

"I'm here. You're okay. All you have to do is—"

"I can't. Whatever you're going to say, I can't. I'm terrified of heights. I always have been."

He didn't say anything for so long that she had begun to fear he'd left her. And why shouldn't he? She was too much of a coward to save her own life.

She had almost given up hope when Ethan spoke again, his voice still soothing. "Raine, I'm coming out there. I'll speak to you before I touch you. Then I'll take your hand and lead you back to the window."

He sounded as if he were talking to a child. And in this situation, she was. She had reverted to the mindless, unreasoning fears of childhood. She had just told him that she'd rather try to cling to the wall behind her than to take the few short steps that would bring her to safety.

"All you'll have to do is hold on to my hand and move sideways with me. Can you do that?"

If he was coming for her, she could. All she had to do was wait for him. And not do anything stupid.

"Yes," she said, forcing agreement through stiff lips. And then her mouth opened again to add, "But hurry, Ethan. *Please* hurry."

Even as she implored him, she could hear him moving along the ledge. If it was wide enough for him to maneuver, then she could manage it. Obviously she'd done it once, which meant she could do it again. The promise of safety and Ethan's arms holding her were surely incentive enough.

She didn't even question the fact that she wanted him to

hold her. That had been the only thing she had known for certain would happen tonight.

She had known she would end up in Ethan Snow's arms before the evening was over. She had thought it would be when they were back in the suite, a far more intimate encounter than this one would be—

"Raine?"

He was so near she could feel his breath against her cheek, just as when he'd leaned close to her at dinner to check out the table behind them. She squeezed her eyes shut, fighting the urge to turn into his arms.

After they were safe. After they were off the ledge.

"I'm going to put my hand on your arm now." His voice was amazingly calm, still reassuring, as his fingers fastened around her wrist. "Okay?"

"Yes."

The word was barely above a whisper. She concentrated on the warmth of his fingers against the coldness of her skin. Just as when he'd taken her hand at dinner tonight and she'd felt the seductive movement of his thumb across the back of it.

"I've got you now. We're going to ease along the ledge. You do exactly what you did before."

Except she couldn't remember what she'd done before. She couldn't remember *doing* this before. Not any part of it.

"I'm not going to let you fall," he went on, his voice still soothing. "Don't even think about it. Just think about taking one step at a time."

One step at a time. Almost before she had time to register the instructions, there was a slight pressure on the arm he held.

In response, she moved her left foot, sliding it along the ledge until she encountered his. For some reason, despite his nearness, she hadn't expected that. She jumped, causing a reflexive tightening of his fingers.

"Easy," he said. "Slide your left foot, then bring the right to meet it. There's no hurry."

As obedient as the child she seemed to have become, she slid her right foot beside her left. He moved again, drawing her with him. Slowly, each step deliberate and precise, he brought her closer and closer to safety.

After an eternity of inching carefully along, her back still pressed against the wall, he said, "We're at the balustrade around the window. Almost there."

Balustrade? She had no idea what he meant. She had no recollection of a balustrade. Of course, she had no recollection of how she had gotten out of the window, either.

"I don't understand."

For a few seconds he didn't answer her. And when he did, her heart sank. "I'm going to leave you while I climb over the rail. All you have to do is stand right here and not move."

"Don't."

She hated the pleading note in her voice, but she couldn't seem to be able to help it. The thought of the loss of contact between them was devastating.

"Ten seconds. Maybe less. I'll climb over and then I'll take your arm again and help you over. All you have to do is not move until I tell you to. Don't breathe. Don't do anything."

He didn't give her time to refuse. Coward that she was, she might have tried to cling to him if he had. The compulsion to try to keep him beside her was almost unbearable.

She sank her teeth into her bottom lip instead and again closed her eyes so she couldn't look down. She listened to the brush of his clothing against stone and then the thud as he jumped down on the other side of the railing apparently now separating them.

"Ready?"

She had no idea what he was going to ask her to do, but whatever it was, it was preferable to spending another second out here alone. A car horn blared somewhere below, reminding her of the alternative to clearing this last hurdle.

"I'm ready," she whispered.

This time his hand took her arm and put it around his neck. "Hold on," he said.

Her fingers gripped the fabric of his tuxedo jacket. He leaned forward so that his cheek was against her hair, his chest pressing hers, as he slipped his arm between the small of her back and the wall. From the angle of his body she knew his torso was extended over the railing she would have to climb across.

"When I tell you," he said, his warm breath feathering over the cold skin of her throat, "lift your other arm and put it around my neck. Once you have a firm hold, turn toward me and find the edge of the balcony with your *right* foot. There's a lip on the outside of the balustrade that's at least three inches wide. All you have to do is get a toehold on that, and I'll pull you over."

Not daring to look down, she tried to visualize the balcony and the lip he'd described. She couldn't believe that she remembered nothing about either, despite the fact that she must have navigated them to get out on the ledge.

"Okay, put your arm around my neck."

She wasn't sure she would have been able to do that without the security of his arm around her back. She could feel its muscles tense in preparation for receiving her weight. He must have taken hold of some part of the balcony with his left hand so that he wouldn't overbalance when he tried to lift her, causing them both to fall.

She stretched out her right arm and put it over his shoulder, grasping him as tightly as she could. His neck was in the crook of her other elbow, her cheek pressed against his.

All she had to do was complete the half turn she'd already begun and find the toehold he'd told her about with her right foot. She tried to pivot on her left foot but the high-heeled sandal she wore refused to budge. Its narrow heel had gotten caught between two of the stones from which the ledge was constructed.

Although the shoe wouldn't give, it was impossible to stop her body's momentum. The strap broke under the strain, letting her foot slide off the sole of the sandal.

She managed to tighten her hold around Ethan's neck as her body swung away from the wall. Frantically she tried to find the toehold he'd told her about with her right foot.

The toe of her other shoe hit something and then slipped off before she could get any traction. There was a heart-stopping, stomach-clenching drop. It couldn't have been more than inches, but it felt like miles while it was happening.

With a grunt of effort, Ethan held on as the full weight of her body dangled a dozen stories off the ground. She had no idea how long he could support her with only one arm and the muscles of his neck and shoulders.

With her feet below the edge of the balcony, she could do little to help. Despite her terror, she knew that now if she swung her legs in an effort to encounter some outcropping, she might unbalance him.

Slowly, with an effort that was communicated through every taut, straining muscle in his arm and torso, Ethan began to pull her up. Inch by brutal inch, he dragged her up, the delicate lace bodice of her dress ripped by the rough concrete of the balustrade.

"Railing," Ethan gasped into her ear.

Despite the restriction of her skirt, she lifted her knee high enough to locate the flat top of the balustrade. When she did, in a matter of seconds Ethan had pulled her across it.

Despite the fact that she was safe, she clung to him, both arms around his neck, her face pressed into his shoulder. They were both trembling, for different reasons, of course.

She could feel his heart thudding against hers. His raced with the exertion; hers with sheer, unmitigated terror.

His arms seemed to be holding as tightly as she was clinging to his neck. After a moment he began to lower her until her toes made contact with the concrete balcony.

She had been relatively unaware of the intimacy of their position until then. In those few seconds, during which her body had slid downward along the length of his, their relationship had crossed some invisible line.

Shocked by her discovery, she realized that relief over the success of her rescue wasn't the only emotion Ethan was feeling. She leaned back, increasing the distance between them enough that she could look up into his face. Shadowed, it appeared as strained as the tired muscles that trembled against hers.

''Through the window,'' he ordered, his voice harsh.

Raine knew it wasn't anger she heard, but she responded as if it were. She removed her arms from around his neck and stepped back. Then, without a word, she squeezed by him and climbed through the window.

Once inside, she looked back at the man outside in the moonlight. Unmoving, he was looking at the ledge on which she'd just been standing.

As she watched, he turned, meeting her eyes. His lips thinned to a straight line before he, too, climbed across the windowsill, following her inside.

Chapter Eleven

"She claims to have no memory of how she got out there," Ethan said. "All she can tell me is it would be the last place she'd go willingly. The only thing that makes sense to me is if she were following some kind of post-hypnotic suggestion."

"Are you suggesting mind control?" Griff's disbelief resounded clearly through the cell phone.

"I know how far-fetched it sounds, but I can't think of anything else that would explain how a woman could climb over a railing and walk out onto on a narrow ledge a hundred feet above the ground and not remember it."

"I can think of several. Drugs. Insanity. The voices made me do it." Griff's list was brief and biting.

"She couldn't have made that climb if she were drugged. And she isn't insane, so unless those 'voices' were giving a post-hypnotic signal…"

"She was standing right beside you before she disappeared. Did you hear anything that *might* have been a trigger?"

Griff's skepticism about the scenario Ethan had outlined was as blatant as that he'd expressed during his interrogation of Raine. Being on the receiving end made Ethan realize how tiresome it must be to constantly be doubted.

If Griff could come up with a more plausible explanation for what had happened tonight, he would welcome it, but he wasn't buying the ones his boss had proposed. Ethan had been there. Griff Cabot hadn't.

"If the suggestion has already been implanted, then the signal that precipitates the action can be anything," Ethan explained. "Music, any other sound, a gesture, color."

"You're saying that she heard or saw something downstairs that caused her to go up to a dark balcony alone, climb through a window and then out onto a ledge."

"I don't know *what* caused her to do any of that. I'm simply trying to find a rational explanation for what occurred. Raine doesn't remember why she left the ballroom or how she got out on the ledge. She has no memory of anything after Steiner called us over to introduce us to his party."

"Carl Steiner? Do you mean he was there? At a charity function?" Griff's inflection had risen with each question.

"Front and center. With several people he insisted I meet. No one I recognized, by the way. You sound surprised. Would that be unusual? Steiner being at tonight's affair?"

"Let's just say that I've never known Carl to be moved by altruistic motives. Not of any kind. And that was the moment Raine disappeared? When Carl called you over?"

Ethan knew Griff had used her first name because *he* had done so. That was the way he thought of her now. As Raine.

Despite the fact that he had acknowledged his attraction from the first, he hadn't realized how strong his feelings had grown until he'd seen her on that ledge tonight. The few seconds during which she had seemed to be slipping out of his grip were the longest—and the most terrifying—of his life.

"One minute her hand was on my arm; the next she was gone."

"Did Steiner know?"

"I didn't see any reason to keep it from him. He tried to be helpful." Ethan mentally recreated his impression of the assistant deputy director's attitude during those crucial seconds. "In retrospect he didn't seem too concerned. By the way, he recognized her name when I introduced them. And he was definitely interested in meeting her. You know that look he has whenever he's trying to figure out how he can use something to his advantage?"

There was little that went on in the capital that escaped the agency's notice. They would certainly have known about the attack on Montgomery Gardner.

Since she'd been part of the CIA's experiments in parapsychology, they probably had an file on Raine, which might even include the claim about her paternity she'd made at the hospital. That would certainly explain Steiner's fascination.

"I mentioned her to him this afternoon," Griff said. "The request I made for information about her was probably the basis for Carl's interest."

"Did you get the records?" Ethan asked. He knew Griff had intended to track down the files on those long-ago CIA experiments in parapsychology, particularly any that contained references to Raine.

"If there ever was a file on something called Cassandra, it no longer exists."

"If there *was* a file?"

"Most of the material on remote viewing was released a few years ago under the Freedom of Information Act. Although it's heavily redacted, there's nothing in it about Ms. McAllister. Or Project Cassandra."

"Are you saying she was wrong about the name? Or just that there isn't any reference to that particular part of it?"

Ethan's understanding was that the research into the paranormal had been extensive. The part Raine had participated in, the remote viewing, had been a fraction of the stuff the agency had experimented with.

"When the Cold War wound down, so did the fear that the Russians would accomplish something in the field of psychic activity that might threaten us. Some of the records may have been destroyed when the projects were terminated. That would mean that, as far as the agency was concerned, they contained nothing of value."

"Steiner himself told you that?" It seemed almost too coincidental that Griff would have talked to the assistant deputy director this afternoon, and then he'd show up tonight—at an event he normally wouldn't have attended—and distract Ethan long enough for Raine to disappear.

"He's the one I call if I need information. For some reason, Carl thinks I had a hand in his promotion into my position after my 'retirement.' As a result of that misplaced gratitude, he's been extremely useful through the years."

Not all the Phoenix agents had as high an opinion of Steiner as Griff had. Lucas Hawkins openly despised him, as did Joshua Stone. No one could deny that the man had provided Griff access to the agency's resources on more than one occasion.

"And while you were talking to him, he didn't think to mention he'd be there tonight?" Ethan asked, allowing his own skepticism to show.

"There's no reason he would have. I didn't tell him you'd be in attendance. Or Ms. McAllister. It didn't come up. Frankly, I could never have imagined Carl attending anything like The Covenant's fund-raiser. It seems uncharacteristic."

"Do you think he could have had something to do with what happened tonight?"

There was a brief silence as Griff examined the possibility. "You'd be in a better position to evaluate that than I would. It seems obvious because of the timing of our inquiry and the subsequent attacks that there's a link between The Covenant and what happened to both Monty and Ms. McAllister. Since their original connection was those experiments, it would follow there must be a link between those CIA projects and The Covenant."

"But without any records of Cassandra—" Ethan began.

"Even *without* records there are ways of reconstructing the past. I'm going to try a few. In the meantime..."

Griff's hesitation lasted so long that Ethan finally broke it. "Yes?"

"It's apparent someone believes Ms. McAllister has information that can help us. You have to keep her safe until we can figure out what she knows that even *she* doesn't realize she knows."

ETHAN PUT HIS EAR against the door of Raine's bedroom before he rapped on it gently with the back of his knuckles. He listened for any sound from the other side, wondering if she'd gone to bed. He'd already begun to turn away when the door opened.

Dressed in one of the thick navy robes the hotel provided, and again barefoot, Raine stood in the opening. The light from the room behind her created a halo effect around her dark hair, loosened to fall over her shoulders.

"What is it?" she asked.

"I just wanted to make sure you're all right."

"As opposed to standing outside on a ledge?"

There was enough self-deprecation in the words that

Ethan responded to them with the truth. "*These* windows don't open. I checked them."

Her lips tilted at the corners. "I suppose I should say thank you for that. And I don't sleepwalk, by the way."

"That's good to know."

There was a small, awkward silence.

"I almost forgot," Ethan said, reaching into his pocket. He held up the earring he'd found at the top of the staircase, the diamonds catching the light from the chandelier in the room behind her.

"My great grandmother's earring," Raine said, holding out her hand for it. "I hadn't even realized it was gone until I was undressing. Where did you find it?"

"At the top of the staircase. That's how I knew you really had come up to the balcony."

"So if I hadn't dropped it—"

He might never have gone through those double doors, he thought. Never found the open window. And if he hadn't...

"Thank you," she said, her fingers curling over the jewelry he'd placed in her outstretched hand. "Thank you for everything you did tonight."

She had thanked him profusely after they were both safely inside the window. He'd been embarrassed by her gratitude, since not only was it his dereliction of duty that had allowed her to wander off alone, but also because he had almost let her fall, a thought that still haunted him.

That was part of the reason he'd knocked on her door. Just to see her again. To make sure, as he'd said, that she really was all right. It was shocking how important that had become to his peace of mind.

"Don't," he said. "I screwed up, which is how you ended up in that situation. You don't owe me any thanks for finally doing my job."

"Just doing my job, ma'am." The tilt of her lips had increased until it was almost a real smile.

"That's right," he said stiffly.

He had expected Griff's censure for tonight's unforgivable lapse. Maybe that's what his warning at the end of the conversation had been about—a reminder of all they had to lose if he allowed anything to happen to Raine McAllister.

It was a reminder he didn't need. Not now. And that had nothing to do with his investigation of The Covenant.

"Have you remembered anything else about—" He stopped because the teasing light suddenly went out of her eyes.

"I can't tell you anything other than what I've already said. I don't know how I got there. Or why. And not knowing makes me feel…" She closed her mouth, lips whitened from the pressure she exerted, before she shook her head.

"*Something* must have happened before you went upstairs," he insisted stubbornly. He much preferred his version of what it might have been to Cabot's. "Something that made you decide to leave the ballroom. Maybe something you heard or saw. Or *someone*."

Her head continued that same side-to-side motion as he talked. "Believe me, I'd tell you if I knew why I climbed those stairs. I don't. I think there was something at the top I needed to see, but…I'm not even sure of that. It may be that I feel that way because I want to remember so badly."

"Don't try to force it."

That's what people in books and movies always said. He had no idea whether the advice was valid. For all he knew, trying to force a recollection might be the best way to deal with something like this.

You spend $7.50 on a movie ticket and think you're a psychiatrist.

Maybe that's what she needed. A psychiatrist. A real one. Maybe Griff was right. Maybe she *wasn't* playing with a full deck.

The game analogy produced the memory of something she had told him that, to his pragmatic sensibilities, seemed to reinforce Cabot's hypotheses. She read *Tarot* cards, for God's sake.

And she'd been instrumental in finding lost children all over this nation, he reminded himself. And she was good enough at what she did for the agency all those years ago that Monty Gardner had recommended they consult her. All of which seemed to indicate—

"I'm *not* crazy."

He realized that she been watching his face while those thoughts raced through his brain. Maybe his expression had revealed enough of what he'd been thinking that she felt compelled to issue that denial.

Or maybe she read your mind. She's supposed to be good at that, too.

At least she had been at one time.

"Why did you stop working with the police?"

Her eyes widened slightly at the non sequitur. "I wondered why you or Mr. Cabot didn't ask me that. It's usually the first thing that comes up when I tell people I can't help them. Especially if something they'd heard about one of those cases was why they came to me."

"I'm asking it now."

"I'll tell you—if you tell me why you left the CIA."

That she knew exactly the question to pose in return was disconcerting. Especially since he'd already reached the point of trying to decide how much, if anything, he could accept about her abilities. What he'd read in Griff's folder had been compelling.

"That isn't the issue here."

The corners of her lips tilted again, but this time her mockery wasn't self-directed. However, she didn't pursue the question she'd asked him.

"I couldn't do it anymore," she said simply.

"And you can *choose* to stop? You can turn it off and on at will?"

"It's not quite that simple, but… To a certain extent, I can seek information or I can choose *not* to seek it. I chose not to."

"Even if—" He broke the question he'd begun, realizing how unfair it was.

"Even if a child were involved?" she finished for him.

"I'm sorry. I had no right to ask that."

"No, you don't."

She let the silence build, making no attempt to justify the decision she'd made. And he found he wanted her to. He *needed* her to.

"Raine—"

"I can't change what people think about me. Not even what *you* think. All I can do is live my life as well as I can."

"And you think refusing to help with those cases qualifies as 'living well'?"

His tone was more accusatory than he'd intended. He was sorry for that, but he couldn't be sorry he had asked. Not given how badly he needed to know.

It took her a long time, but at least she didn't do what she had done that first night. She didn't try to close him out.

"I was surprised the cops I had worked with understood. And I would have thought that if anyone else in this world *could* understand—"

This time she was the one who broke off a sentence that might have inflicted irreparable damage to their relationship. *Their relationship?* he questioned. That presupposed they had one. It was always possible that what he felt was completely one-sided. In any case...

"I need to know."

He understood that whatever she told him, even if he couldn't accept it as reason enough for the decision she'd made, would require a reciprocal sharing of information. Maybe she wouldn't be able to accept what he had done, either.

"After years of working on those kinds of cases," she said, "I came to believe that there's a threshold, a limit if you will, to what the human mind can accept of what's out there. I started to fear I was reaching my limit."

"'Of what's out there'?" he repeated.

It took a moment for her to put into words what they both knew this was about. "The evil in the world."

"The evil that abducts children."

"And does unspeakable things to them." Her voice was barely above a whisper.

It was only what he had guessed when she made reference to his reasons for leaving the agency. "You felt you'd seen too much of it."

"I'm not sure of the context in which you're using that word, but...it wasn't seeing it that was the most disturbing."

"I don't understand."

"I felt it."

"Their evil?"

"That. Their madness. And the other. All the other."

He had never considered that aspect of what she did. It put everything into a new and sickening light.

"You felt what they felt? The children?"

She nodded, her eyes glazing with moisture for the first

time since he had known her. She blinked quickly, clearing them as if she were embarrassed to let that emotion show.

"If they were still alive."

"Dear God," he whispered.

Her smile this time was bitter and twisted. "If He could allow things like that—"

"Raine."

"I know. I've told myself that a thousand times. Men *choose* good or evil. We all do. I chose good for as long as I could, but in doing that, I learned far too much about the other. I had to step back and let someone else fight that battle. It was either that or—"

"I know." He did know. Perhaps better than she could ever understand.

He put his hand on her cheek, allowing his palm to shape the line of her jaw. With his thumb he touched her lips, trying to tell her how sorry he was for making her talk about this. After a moment he leaned forward to press a kiss on her forehead.

When he stepped back, her eyelids were closed, the long lashes motionless against her cheeks. Her eyes opened slowly to look up into his.

He fought the urge to put his lips against the place his thumb had brushed. That would happen eventually. He knew it as surely as if he were the one with the gift.

"That's what I felt tonight."

Her whispered words were so far from what he'd been thinking that it took him a moment to make sense of them.

"Evil?"

"The unspeakable kind that thinks nothing of anyone else's suffering. The kind that's unable to imagine how suffering feels. And wouldn't care if it could. It was so strong it terrified me."

"At dinner?"

She nodded.

"That's what you felt from the tables behind us?"

Another nod, her eyes still on his.

"The man who called me over—"

"Carl Steiner." She had supplied the name before he could even complete the question and then she went on to answer it. "He's...ruthless," she said, seeming to choose her words with care. "And he knows a lot about me. More than he wanted you to know, but..." She shook her head. "What I felt tonight didn't come from him. His interest is like a scientist with a new bug to dissect. The other—"

"Tell me," he demanded when she hesitated.

"The other was that same madness. In this case a very organized, focused madness. Far more ruthless than Steiner ever thought about being."

"Could it have been someone who was with him?"

Those people should be easy enough to check. He remembered a couple of the names, and with Griff's help—

"I don't think so, but I can't be sure. I didn't touch any of them. I didn't look into their eyes. Besides..."

"Besides what?"

"If what I felt came from someone who was with Steiner, then we're left with the same unanswered question."

"I don't understand."

"If that feeling originated from someone who was standing next to us, then why in the world would I have gone up those stairs to the balcony?"

Chapter Twelve

She wasn't sure why Ethan had come to her door. Maybe simply to ask her again the questions for which she still had no answers. Why she'd gone upstairs. And, more important, why she'd gone out on the ledge.

Without those two pieces of the puzzle…

"Maybe in the morning things will seem clearer," he'd said before he left. "Maybe while you sleep, your subconscious will remember something that can explain what happened tonight."

Since the only other occasion on which she had lost time was the first night she'd seen the image of the pond, she had no experience to guide her. What she felt right now was that the black void that hid both her actions and her motives was impenetrable.

"Maybe," she'd said noncommittally.

There was another of those awkward pauses before he had nodded. "I'll see you tomorrow then. Sleep well."

She wouldn't. She knew that as surely as she knew that she had nothing more to fear tonight. Of course, she hadn't felt any sense of anxiety about the function they'd attended, either.

All she had felt as she'd dressed was anticipation. Not about what would happen at the dinner, but about what she knew would happen when they returned to the hotel. To this suite.

And she'd been wrong.

The lack of foreknowledge since she'd been in Washington had never happened before. It confused her, making her doubt something that had once been as natural as breathing.

As a child she had believed that everyone knew the things she knew. When it would rain. What someone was really thinking, despite what they said. The days her mother was going to be too sick to get up in the morning, leaving her to her own devices. Not that she ever minded that.

There was a whole world to explore. A world that consisted not only of the sights and sounds everyone saw, but her world, rich with the color and texture of thoughts and emotions.

Some of those had been dark, a little frightening to the child she had been then. It had taken her a long time to encounter real evil, however, which was far more rare than most people believed.

And when she had finally learned the taste and smell and feel of it, she had chosen to protect herself in the only way she knew how. She had chosen to deny the ability she had been born with.

And now, when, for the first time in her life, she needed the gifts with which to protect *herself,* they were no longer hers to command.

A punishment for having denied them? Or the natural result of attempting to stifle the sensations that had once bombarded her with images and emotions, like some psychic Fourth of July fireworks display?

Whatever its cause, the effect seemed certain. What she anticipated was no longer a reliable guide to what would happen. And she could encounter people like the man at the hospital and not be aware of the danger he represented until it was too late.

Which brought into question her ability to sense other people's motivations. She had told Ethan that the evil she'd been aware of tonight had not emanated from Carl Steiner. What if she were wrong about that? Just as she had been wrong about what she had thought would occur between her and Ethan.

If she *were* wrong about Steiner, what would be the consequences? Consequences that would affect not only her, but the man who had just crossed the suite to return to his bedroom.

She glanced up and realized that without any clear idea of how she had gotten there, she was standing in front of one of the windows overlooking the city. Although the penthouse suite was too high to allow her to hear the traffic, the scene below was not so different from what she had glimpsed during those terrifying minutes she'd spent edging along that ledge. And she had no more idea how she had reached this point than she had about how she had gotten out there tonight.

Was she losing her mind? Had the thing she had always feared more than any other finally happened? Had evil, which had been her adversary since she'd accepted that what she could do was almost unique, finally won?

Determinedly pushing that thought out of her head, she reached up to pull the heavy draperies across the expanse of glass. For an instant before the curtain hid it from sight, the sheen of its surface had been as cold and dark and opaque as the pond in her vision.

ETHAN WAS STANDING in front of the windows in his bedroom, looking unseeingly out on the capital's landmarks when his cell rang. He stepped over to the bed where he'd tossed the phone while he'd undressed and picked it up on the second ring.

"Snow."

"I've arranged a meeting here in my office for you and Ms. McAllister in the morning at ten," Griff Cabot said. "I assume she has nothing planned for tomorrow."

"Like a little casual shopping maybe? If she does, she didn't mention it to me."

He knew he shouldn't be offended at the tone of Cabot's question. Griff hadn't been out on that ledge tonight when he'd almost let her fall. What had happened to Raine hadn't been the result of Cabot's inattention.

"How's she doing?" Reacting to his sarcasm perhaps, Cabot managed to eject both compassion and concern into the inquiry.

"Probably as well as anyone could be who's been through that kind of frightening experience. Especially someone who has no explanation for it."

"That isn't your problem."

"I know. My problem is making sure nothing like that happens again. At least, not until we can determine what she knows."

He could almost feel Cabot evaluating the tone of that last sentence. How well he had was evidenced by his next comment.

"Don't get emotionally involved, Ethan. That's advice from a friend, by the way."

"As opposed to being from the head of the Phoenix and my boss?"

"I've never had much success ordering my operatives to avoid emotional entanglements. I *have* had my share of trouble in dealing with them."

"She told me why she stopped working child abductions."

Maybe he wanted Cabot to ask. Or maybe he had just wanted him to know some of what he was finally beginning to understand about Raine McAllister—the burden and the curse her so-called gift had always been.

And that presumes you believe she has one.

He had, he realized. At least during those few moments when she had talked about encountering the real evil in the world. He had seen enough of it to know at a level far deeper than the intellectual exactly what she had meant.

"I think we all can appreciate what working those kinds of cases—"

"We may *think* we appreciate it. She *experienced* it, Griff. All of it. All the things that were done to those children. She felt what they felt. We can't possibly *appreciate* that."

The accusatory words were out before he remembered that Griff's baby daughter had been kidnapped. Cabot had a better understanding of the terror that kind of situation generated than most people. Certainly better than he had.

"I'm sorry," Ethan said quickly. "I'd forgotten about your daughter. I didn't mean—"

"I know what you meant," Cabot said brusquely. "I take it that you believed her. You think she's an empath."

Ethan had never heard that word used outside the realm of science fiction. If Raine could really do what she had claimed tonight, however...

"I don't know what she is. All I know is that when she told me about the children... I *knew* she was telling the truth."

"As she understands it," Cabot said.

"What the hell does that mean?"

"It means I'd be interested in testing Ms. McAllister. If she really believes she's able to do the things that she's been credited with, she shouldn't object to undergoing some kind of objective evaluation.''

''Maybe we could just point to a place on the map and ask her to describe what's there.''

His anger over what Raine had endured as a child must have come through loud and clear. Maybe she wouldn't object to an evaluation, but Ethan knew he would. It was just another form of exploitation. As was what *they* were doing to her.

''We went to her,'' he reminded Cabot. ''She made no claims about her ability. Actually, she said all along she couldn't help us.''

''She already has.''

''How?''

''What happened tonight proves we're on the right track. And so was Monty.''

On the right track…

The phrase keyed a memory. Something he hadn't told Cabot. The thing that had let him know he was on the right track in his search tonight. Maybe it wasn't significant, but he'd been trained that every detail was important in a debriefing, and this was something he'd forgotten to mention.

''That reminds me. There was something I didn't tell you about the dinner. It had slipped my mind until I was undressing tonight.''

''Yes?'' Cabot sounded slightly impatient.

''It's probably not important, but it's how I knew Raine really had gone up to the balcony, despite the fact that Steiner suggested otherwise.''

''I thought you saw her.''

''I wasn't sure. Not sure enough to search the entire balcony. Not until I found one of the earrings she'd been wearing.''

The silence on the other end of the line suddenly seemed thick. Pregnant with anticipation.

"An earring?" Griff said finally.

"She said they had belonged to her great-grandmother. I'm not sure how to explain it, given the darkness at the top of the stairs, but somehow the stones caught what light was there. As soon as I noticed the earring, I knew she was on the balcony. I kept looking until I found the open window and the cloak I told you about. And then…I found her."

If he hadn't, who knew how long she could have stayed out there without falling. Or maybe she'd been programmed to do that, too. To close her eyes and lean forward—

"Her great-grandmother's earring."

Griff's inflection had not been questioning, but Ethan could think of no other way to interpret the phrase.

"That's right."

"Interesting."

Once more he was unable to read Cabot's tone. There seemed to be something going on under the surface of their conversation. Something he didn't understand. It was a feeling he'd experienced once too often tonight.

"As I said, it was nothing important, but I wanted to—" Suddenly it hit him why Griff might be interested in jewelry Raine claimed had belonged to her great-grandmother. "She didn't say which side of the family."

"No, I'm sure she wouldn't," Cabot said, his voice tinged with what sounded like amusement. "I'll see you both here at ten. That, too, should be interesting."

Before Ethan could think of a suitable response, the connection was broken. He thought about calling Griff back, but instead he pitched the phone onto the bed again and returned to the windows.

He hadn't even thought to ask who the meeting tomorrow was with. Someone Griff believed would provide a test of Raine's abilities or someone from her past. In either case, someone Ethan knew he would want to protect her from.

Griff was right. It would be far better if he weren't emotionally involved with Raine McAllister. And far too late to do anything about the fact that he was.

Chapter Thirteen

Raine told herself she shouldn't be surprised by the second knock on her door. It was only vindication. Despite the strength of her earlier feeling that something was going to happen between them tonight, however, she hadn't expected Ethan to return.

She picked up the robe she'd thrown on the foot of her bed, belting it around her waist as she hurried toward the door. Before she allowed her fingers to close around the knob, she took a breath, trying to quell her anticipation.

When she opened the door and saw him standing outside, a surge of sweet, hot heat rushed through her lower body. He had discarded the jacket of his tux as well as the tie. His pleated evening shirt was open at the throat, revealing a tantalizing glimpse of dark hair against bronzed skin.

"What's wrong?" she asked, pushing the words out past the sudden dryness in her throat.

"Cabot called. He's arranged a meeting for us at ten in the morning. I thought I should warn you."

The word seemed ominous, but maybe she was reading more into them than he'd intended. It was already late. Maybe he simply wanted to tell her to leave a wake-up call.

"A meeting with whom?"

"I honestly didn't think to ask."

She could sense his embarrassment over the admission. "That's all right. I don't suppose it makes any difference."

"Probably someone connected to the remote viewing experiments. Griff's been trying to gather information about them, but the agency's stonewalling him about the records. Even without them, his sources are very good."

"Thanks for the warning. What time should I be ready?"

"Since it's a Sunday, it shouldn't take more than half an hour to get to the office."

"Nine-fifteen?"

He nodded. Neither of them moved for a few seconds, their eyes holding.

"Well, good night," he said finally, beginning to turn away from the door.

"Ethan?"

The sound of his name stopped the motion he'd begun. And what she saw in his eyes as he looked back was the same emotion that was in her heart.

"Don't go."

He studied her face a moment before he said, "There's nothing for you to be afraid of. Not here."

"I'm not afraid."

A heartbeat of silence.

"Then… What's wrong?"

She smiled at him, a little bemused at how difficult this was proving to be. "I must have forgotten how this is done. Or is it that you're just not interested?"

His head tilted as if he were questioning what she'd just said. "If you mean…" He hesitated, still holding her eyes. "I don't think this is a good idea. Not with what's been going on."

It was obviously rejection, no matter how it was phrased. Her stomach tightened with disappointment. Given the clarity of what she had felt about where their relationship was headed, she didn't allow herself to be deterred by it. There had to still be *some* advantages to the gift she'd been given.

"I thought you were supposed to keep an eye on me," she said. "I thought that was part of your job."

Just doing my job, ma'am.

"Not a literal eye." His voice had softened.

"And if I asked you to do that? To keep a 'literal eye' on me?"

"If you're afraid that what happened at the hotel—"

"That *isn't* what's going to happen tonight."

Another beat of silence. "You sound very sure of that."

She didn't reiterate her certainty. Her smile, however, undoubtedly revealed it.

Seeing it, he asked, "What happened to the business about everyone having free choice?"

"You have free choice."

"Like hell."

The words were whispered as he leaned forward to claim her lips. His head had tilted so that their mouths were aligned at the perfect angle. His fastened over hers with an expertise that was exactly what she had expected. There was no awkwardness. No hesitation.

His tongue demanded entrance. And since she had no desire to deny him anything, her mouth opened willingly to receive it.

As he kissed her, his fingers found the knot of the belt that held her robe together. They made quick work of it, allowing the two sides to fall apart. She was aware of the small intake of breath that signaled his discovery that she'd been wearing nothing beneath it.

His hands settled over the indention of her waist, their palms, slightly callused, sensually abrasive against her skin. Suddenly, as if he couldn't wait, he pulled her to him, crushing her breasts against the muscled wall of his chest. She could feel the strength of his erection against her stomach.

His hands slipped lower still, curving over the roundness of her hips. He lifted until his arousal was pressed against her lower body. Far more demanding than his lips or his tongue had been.

· She put her arms around his neck, standing on tiptoe to continue the deepening kiss. As she did, there was an unwanted flashback to the instant on the ledge when her foot had turned and she had literally been hanging on to him for dear life. In response to the memory her body stiffened.

Ethan pulled back, raising his head slightly to break the kiss. She opened her eyes to find him looking down into her face. Questioning.

"It's nothing," she said, stretching upward to reestablish contact with his lips.

Without his muscled warmth against her bare skin, the air from the climate-controlled suite was uncomfortably cool. As she tried to move back into his embrace, his hands found her shoulders, holding her away from him a little.

"If this is intended to be some form of thanks..."

"I don't pay my debts like this." Her use of the phrase was deliberate, and it stopped him, just as she'd intended.

"I didn't mean to imply that I thought this was some kind of payment. It's natural after an experience like tonight's—"

"That I'd throw myself into your arms and suggest we make mad, passionate love?"

Another hesitation as he examined what she'd said.

"Is that what you're doing?"

"Well, it's certainly what I'm *trying* to do. I don't seem to be having much success."

"Why?"

"Because you're stubborn?" she suggested. "Or too noble for your own good maybe."

"I didn't mean that. I meant why are you doing this?"

"Because I want you to make love to me," she said patiently, as if she were explaining this to a child.

"You barely know me."

She smiled, thinking how shocked he'd be to realize how very well she did know him.

"Don't tell me you didn't sense this was inevitable."

Again her words gave him pause. But at least he answered them truthfully.

"I knew there was something between us."

"But you'd rather play it out. Do you need to be courted, Mr. Snow?"

"Not usually."

"Then why in the world would you—? Oh," she said, finally understanding his reluctance.

She tried to think if she'd ever made love to another man who knew as much about her as this one did. Not that there had been such a number of intimate encounters in her past. There were, after all, distinct drawbacks in being able to gauge intentions and to discern the truth behind what people said.

"You're afraid I'm going to read your mind."

"Are you?"

"Not if you don't want me to. But…there *could* be advantages to that. Something you might want to think about."

Again his head tilted—questioning—but she could tell his discomfort with the idea had begun to fade. He had known this was inevitable.

She stepped forward, finding the button that held the waistband of his pants. She slipped it free of the buttonhole and then slid the zipper down. Held up by the black sus-

penders, the pants didn't move. Not that she'd intended
them to.

She untucked the tail of the evening shirt and began removing the studs that fastened it. At least he was no longer
asking questions, she thought as she worked with single-
minded determination.

When she reached the last of them, she glanced up and
found his eyes on her face. In the dimness of the hallway,
their gray was so dark it was almost black.

For an instant, a flutter of fear brushed through her mind.
At some point tonight she had looked up into another pair
of eyes, blacker even than these. Those had been cold, however. Cold and black, just like the pond in her vision.

Her hand hesitated as she tried to recapture the fleeting
memory. It was no use. Whatever she had almost remembered had again disappeared from her mind.

And since she had other memories to make—far more
inviting than the bone-chilling sensation that one produced—she let go of the small, worrisome recollection. She
didn't want to think about anything that had ever happened
before this moment. This encounter.

When she had removed the last stud, she pushed the shirt
down over Ethan's shoulders, revealing the sleeveless undershirt he wore beneath it. In comparison to the long elegance of his torso, his shoulders and upper arms seemed
heavily muscled.

Thank God, she thought, remembering the endless strain
they'd endured until he had been able to pull her to safety.

She bent forward, putting her lips against the semicircle
of tanned skin revealed by the low neck of the undershirt.
At the same time she pushed the evening shirt further down
his arms until it fell onto the dark, patterned carpet.

Ethan stepped back, ripping the undershirt off over his

head in a single motion. Balling it in one hand, he lobbed it toward the couch in the living room of the suite.

Before it landed, he had stepped forward again, pulling her back into his arms. This time there was no barrier between her breasts and the hair-roughened skin of his chest. Her breath caught in her throat as his hands closed over her hips, lifting her once more against his erection.

"There's a bed," she whispered.

"I never figured you for conventional."

His lips were pressed against her ear. A jolt of pure sensation shot through her body as his tongue slipped inside to rim the outer shell.

"It isn't *where* you make love that determines if you're conventional," she said. "It's how."

"I have a few ideas about that."

His breath stirred against the moisture his tongue had left, causing her to shiver. In response, his arms tightened around her, holding her close.

"I know," she said.

He raised his head, looking down into her eyes, the unspoken question in his. Instead of answering it, she smiled at him.

"Exactly what is it that you know?" he asked.

"That it's going to be incredible," she said truthfully.

THE BED HAD BEEN TURNED DOWN. And although the lamps on either side of the headboard were on, the light they provided was very dim. From somewhere came the soft sound of good jazz.

All the elements of seduction were in place, Ethan noted. Including her nudity under the hotel bathrobe.

Of course, she had made no secret of her intent from the first. How she had known he'd come knocking on her door, however...

"Ethan?"

Only when she said his name did he realize that he'd come to a stop just across the threshold. She took his hand, smiling at him again. He allowed her to draw him closer to the center of the room, dominated by the king-size bed.

Despite the time they'd spent talking in the doorway, a hint of steam lingered in the air from what must have been a very recent shower. It was redolent of bath oil or soap, which had been scented with the same perfume she'd worn tonight.

The fragrance produced a mental picture of Raine, holding her hair off her neck with one hand as she turned under those powerful jets, allowing them to ease the tension in her neck and shoulders. And then allowing them to play over her breasts as she lathered her body, leaving behind the subtle aroma that was driving him wild.

Apparently she isn't the only one who has visions.

Visions. Clairvoyance. CIA.

The progression was natural. And it stopped the one he'd been making across her bedroom.

When it did, she turned back. "Is something wrong?"

"I'm not sure this is a good idea."

Griff was right. Becoming emotionally involved in any case was dangerous. It was exactly what had led to his leaving the agency, only in that case he had been in emotional overload because of the death of a fellow agent. Not just his death, he amended, but the manner of his dying.

Given his background, becoming emotionally involved with a woman he was supposed to be protecting was more than dangerous. It was foolish. Especially with a woman who was essential to their understanding of the connection between those CIA experiments and The Covenant.

"What can I do to convince you?" Still holding his hand, Raine moved closer, smiling into his eyes.

"I'm here to protect you. *Not* to sleep with you."

The stiff-necked bureaucratic jerk was back. With a vengeance.

"Because you'll have to report it to Griff if you do?"

"Because it blurs the lines between personal and professional."

"Yes, it would," she said, her smile widening.

"I'm not sure I'd be comfortable with that. I'm not sure you should be, either."

"We're both adults. Consenting adults, I assume. And I also assume you wouldn't be the first of Cabot's agents to become personally involved with a client."

The last agent who had done so had lost his position with the Phoenix. It wasn't really that Ethan was afraid of losing his. It was more a matter of trust. Griff had entrusted him with Raine's safety. To be her bodyguard, not her lover.

Even the word as it formed in his mind was tempting. Almost as much so as the sight of her nude body, partially revealed by the unbelted robe.

"I wouldn't be the first," he conceded. "Despite that, I owe Griff a greater debt than some of the others. That means I don't betray his trust."

"Because he accepted you into the Phoenix."

"*After* I left the CIA. Something he tried to talk me out of."

"If anyone could understand your reasons for leaving, I would think it would be Cabot."

Although he hadn't told her his reasons, this was the second time she had acted as if she knew them. Even if she did, they were not something he wanted to get into tonight.

Just as he didn't want to be having this conversion. All he wanted—

All he wanted, he realized, was to carry her over to the big bed and make love all night. A hell of an admission for a man who had just been arguing the opposite point of view for the past five minutes.

"It's up to you," she said, her tone carefully neutral. "I should warn you, though, that even if it doesn't happen tonight, it will eventually."

"But you thought it would tonight."

"Yes."

"Does that mean the things you foresee don't always come to pass?"

"I don't 'foresee' that many things," she said carefully. "Occasionally, however, the sense that something is about to happen is so strong it's just there."

"Like this?"

"Yes."

"But you didn't know about the other."

"The ledge? I had no inkling about that. And I know what you're thinking."

He doubted it. All he seemed capable of thinking about right now was that wide expanse of bed behind her.

"I have no explanation for why I didn't," she went on. "All I can tell you is that when I was dressing tonight, I *knew* you were going to make love to me. The other..."

She shrugged. The movement lifted her shoulders beneath the robe, causing the opening to separate. Almost unconsciously she pulled the two sides together again, looping one end of the belt through the other.

Ethan's hands closed over hers. Surprised, she looked up, her eyes wide.

"Don't," he said. She had asked if he needed to let this play out. Apparently, *she* didn't.

She didn't try to be coy or to tease him about the fact that he couldn't seem to make his emotions align with his intellect. Instead, she loosened the loop she'd just made, allowing the robe to fall open again.

This time he reached up, and as she had with his shirt, he pushed the garment off her shoulders. It fell, but she made no attempt to cover herself.

Reality matched to perfection the image of Raine in the shower that the hint of her perfume had conjured up a moment ago. And he'd even been right about the tan. It definitely hadn't been acquired while wearing a swimsuit.

Taking his time, he examined the smooth shoulders and the small, perfect globes of her breasts. Then his gaze slowly trailed lower. Across a flat stomach with a small teardrop-shaped naval. Down long, slender legs, toned from swimming or running on the beach. Bare, high-arched feet.

Attempting to regain some control, he looked up again, meeting her eyes. Tonight they were pure blue, shining like the heat in the heart of a flame.

She smiled at him, her lips curving in what could only be an invitation. One that, God help him, he didn't have the strength to refuse.

She held out her hand, palm flattened. Before the thought of why this was wrong could intrude again, he placed his fingers on top of hers, his thumb curling around them tightly.

Then, because just as she had, he had known this was inevitable, he allowed her to lead him to the bed that had beckoned since he'd entered the room. Right or wrong, he was totally incapable of turning back now.

Chapter Fourteen

"Here. And here."

He closed his eyes again, trying to regain some shred of control. Some vestige of sanity. He would ultimately lose this battle—just as he had earlier—but his pride refused to let him surrender without a fight.

He had intended to make love to Raine. Of course, there was an old axiom about the road to hell being paved with good intentions. In this case it had proven to be the road to Heaven instead.

He eased a breath, trying to still the growing clamor in his body. To stem the rising tide of molten heat that was flooding his veins, filling them with a demand that knew only one release.

He had lost count of the number of times she had brought him to climax. Found it impossible to catalogue the methods she had used.

With her hands, with her lips, teeth and tongue, she had shown him things about his own body and its responses that no other woman had ever evoked.

No other woman...

He was almost mindless with sensation. Drowning in it: And yet every second of every intimacy, he was aware of her. As if, while she physically touched him, she was also infusing her feelings within him.

"And this," she whispered.

In response to what she had just done, the fingers of his right hand closed over the sheet, clenching it. A jolt of sensation lifted his hips off the mattress.

The fingers of his left hand, tangled through the long, silken strands of her hair, had also tightened reflexively before he realized he might be hurting her. With the last ounce of willpower he possessed, he forced them to loosen.

As they did, the flood of sensation he'd fought gained ground against his determination. He knew then that there was no longer anything he could do to prevent what was about to happen.

Nothing except to give in and ride out another incredible experience.

The urge to do so was almost irresistible. Instead, he took another breath, rebuilding control over his body atom by atom. Nerve ending by nerve ending. Inch by inch.

This time… This time…

She touched him again, and the gains he had counted in millimeters were wiped out by a pleasure so intense it literally took his breath. He wasn't even certain what she'd done. He supposed it didn't matter. Not in the grand scheme of things.

Whatever it was had destroyed the last glimmer of restraint. Feeling flared along nerve pathways so sensitized that pleasure verged on pain.

His hips lifted again. His back arched, every muscle stretched hard and tight. His head fell back, the tendons in his neck corded with strain. His mouth opened, trying to pull a breath into aching lungs as the air thinned and darkened around him. Consciousness of the present spiraled away into a void, riding the crest of sensation.

When it was finally over, he could do nothing but lie, limp and exhausted, as the sweat-drenched sheets beneath him grew cold. After an eternity, he opened his eyes to find that Raine was propped above him on one elbow, looking down into his face.

At some point during the night she had turned out the lamps on either side of the bed. The only light in the room was moonlight, which painted one cheek and half her forehead with silver, leaving the other side in shadow. Her eyes were luminous, dark and wide.

"What the hell are you trying to do to me?"

Her lips curved at his question before she leaned forward to place them gently over his. They were cool against his heated skin. Smooth and slightly moist.

"I'm making love to you," she whispered as she straightened. "Do you like it?"

He couldn't conjure up words that would adequately answer that question, so he decided not to try. "I'm supposed to make love to you," he said instead.

"Is that a rule?"

"I always thought so," he admitted, allowing his lips to relax into an answering smile.

He was relieved that she didn't seem disappointed with what was happening between them. After all, she had taken the initiative from the beginning. He'd let her, of course, assuming that their lovemaking would eventually become something more normal.

Normal...

Like an earthquake? Or a nuclear explosion?

She had promised him incredible, and she'd been right. It was just that this was nothing like he'd anticipated. Nothing he *could* have anticipated.

"I've never played by the rules," she said. "Maybe because I never understood them."

"You understand enough."

The corner of her mouth that was visible moved again. "This has nothing to do with rules."

"Maybe with breaking them."

"And you've never been comfortable with that."

Another instance when she seemed to know more about him than she should. He was becoming used to those.

Because she was right, of course. A lot of Griff's operatives had been mavericks and loners, men comfortable with chaos and disorder who, if it hadn't been for Cabot, would have preferred to operate outside the parameters of a team.

He had always been more disciplined, once even believing he could impose order not only upon himself, but also on the world around him. And that by working with Griff's elite counterterrorism team, he could bring justice and freedom to those who had never known it.

He had found instead an international community indifferent to human suffering and to the madmen who caused it. Despite Cabot's efforts, the CIA had eventually restricted the team's actions so much that it was as if they were forced to fight with one hand tied behind their backs. Because of that, good men had died, some in ways he still had nightmares about.

Since he'd left the agency, Ethan had never allowed himself to care enough about anything or anybody to make him vulnerable to that kind of disillusionment. Tonight Raine had broken down all the barriers he had built between himself and anything that could threaten his control. And then she'd accused him of not being comfortable breaking rules.

"I haven't been. Not until tonight," he said.

"I told you there were advantages."

She meant advantages to her gift. Obviously, there were.

He just hadn't realized how many of those would accrue to him.

She lowered the elbow she'd been propped on, lying down beside him again. He put his arm around her back, pulling her to him. She laid her cheek against his shoulder. The palm of her left hand rested flat on the center of his chest, just above his still-rapid heartbeat.

"Is that what you were doing?" he asked. "Reading my mind?"

Every man has fantasies. He was no different from anyone else in that respect. There were certain intimacies he had imagined some beautiful woman performing on his body, but he could never have imagined Raine in that role. Like him, she had seemed to value her control far too much to become a part of someone else's fantasy.

But she had. Every one he'd ever imagined as well as a dozen more he'd never dared to dream. And there could be only one way that this woman—cool, poised, sophisticated—could have known each of his wildest fantasies in such detail.

"I didn't think about it like that," she said. "It was more a matter of wanting to give you pleasure. Trying to think of things that would please you. If they did, it was obvious by your reactions. There was nothing mystical about any of this."

"Speak for yourself," he said, tightening his hold around her slender body.

He could feel the breath of her laughter against the dampness of his skin. Unbelievably, given his exhaustion, a shimmer of sexual heat flickered through his groin.

She must have felt that stirring under the tanned thigh that lay across his lower body. She raised her head a little, looking down at him with a smile.

"Don't start," he warned, provoking another breath of laughter. "Just lie very still."

"Poor baby."

The tone was falsely sympathetic, her amusement at his predicament clear. He ignored it, concentrating on stoking the small, determined blaze that was growing in his body by remembering each diabolically delicious torment she'd inflicted. Now it was payback time, and he didn't intend to be humiliated by his own satiation.

He closed his eyes, imagining a few intimacies of his own. She might be able to anticipate his plans, but she really couldn't do anything about them. Even if she wanted to.

Obediently she put her head back on his shoulder, her fingers idly caressing the hair on his chest. It was enough to fan the spark that had ignited the tinder of his desire. He closed his eyes, thinking about the first of the dozen ways he wanted to bring her to fulfillment.

He had no doubt she would be as responsive to his touch as he had been to hers. The chemistry, as she'd called it, had been there from the moment she'd opened the door of her beach house to him. It had grown with each second they'd spent together, even those when danger had been the motivating force that had drawn them together. Maybe especially during those.

Her eyes, filled with the certainty of what the man at the hospital was capable of. Her arms, clinging to his neck, holding on for dear life.

He opened his eyes, the memory of that terrifying instant when he had felt her slipping away from him too real. Too much of a reminder of the danger she faced.

"What's wrong?"

Her hand still lay on his chest. The leap his heart had taken at that remembrance would have been telling.

Instead of answering, instead of carrying out any of the sexual ploys he had been thinking of, he rolled over, carrying her with him, until she lay under him, pinned by his weight. As he looked down into her face, the arousal he'd been nursing was suddenly full-blown.

The realization of how deeply he had come to care about her shocked him. He didn't bother to deny the truth he'd just discovered, not even to himself.

He didn't want to blurt it out like the schoolboy she always made him feel. It was too sudden. The emotion too uncontrolled. All of the rash, impulsive things he was not.

Before he'd met Raine McAllister.

He looked down into her face, seeing it anew. With new eyes.

There wasn't enough light to find the faint scattering of freckles. There was a smudge of mascara beneath her lashes, and the generous mouth had long ago lost the coating of lip gloss she'd put on for the evening. Her eyes were almost black in the dimness, the pupils wide. Still looking up into his.

And what he read there…

He lowered his head, forgetting those thoughts of sexual payback. His lips found hers instead, gentle as he pressed a series of featherlight kisses along them.

She tried to engage his tongue, but he ignored her demand, playing this his way. And his way right now was to show her the tenderness his newfound realization had created.

Despite what Gardner might have done for her, Raine's life had been difficult, her gift both a blessing and a curse. Even when she had tried to use her abilities for good, the effort had proven to be a two-edged sword.

Her lips slowly opened under his, no longer demanding,

but acquiescing. An unspoken agreement that he was in charge. She had had her turn at control; this was his.

He deepened the kiss, trying to express something of what he felt. Her hand found the back of his head, opened fingers sliding through his hair.

He tightened his hold, wanting to fill her, to own her, to overwhelm her with what he felt for her. Just as his emotions had overwhelmed him.

Her lips clung, her tongue matching the slow, deliberate movements of his. A prelude to what would inevitably follow.

His hand found her breast, cupping under its fullness. He caught the nipple between his fingers, rolling it. A small moan sounded low in her throat.

Unable to resist, he lifted his head, breaking the kiss, and then lowered it again, taking the peak he had teased to tautness into his mouth. He suckled hard, feeling the answering arch and twist of her hips beneath his body.

His teeth closed over flesh, and then his tongue rimmed the softness surrounding the hardened nub before he suckled it again. Her breath released, the exhalation almost a gasp.

Before that sound had faded into the darkness, his mouth had covered hers. At the same time his fingers found the moisture his kiss had created in her lower body. Hot and wet and ready for his entrance.

He used the fluid to touch her, forcing her down the same spiraling pathway where she had driven him. Taking her to the edge of the abyss and then bringing her back.

Controlling her. Feeling her trembling beneath him with need and desire. Exalting in his ability to make her mindless with wanting him. As he had been mindless wanting her.

"Please," she whispered, the word shivering out into the moonlight.

He had fought his own loss of control. Railed against it.

In contrast, she sought its release. Wanted it. Begged him for it.

And this was, after all, what he had wanted, too. To make love to her. To carry her along the path to the same ecstasy where she had led him.

He eased his body over hers. Her eyes opened, looking up into his face. He smiled at her as he touched her, waiting for the exact moment when she would be on the verge of capitulation.

He sensed it first in the trembling of her body. It started as a shiver and then grew until she was shaking as if she were in the throes of fever.

Before the flood could break, he had positioned himself. With one smooth, downward thrust, he entered her. The trembling became a cataclysm, breaking around him.

He drove into her again and again. Her nails marked his shoulders, but he was unaware of pain. Unaware of anything but her hips arching beneath his, matching each stroke until his explosion joined hers.

Tangled together in a web of sensation, they clung to one another until it was over. When it was, unwilling or unable to move, they lay exhausted in its wake.

Still joined. Still connected, both in mind and body. Content in a way he had never been before.

Raine was the first to stir, her fingers again idly caressing the hair on his chest. He put his hand over hers, holding it.

"Good?" For some stupid, schoolboy reason, he needed to hear her say it. To acknowledge that he had in some small way given her back some part of what she had given him.

"You couldn't tell?"

"I don't have your advantages."

She laughed. "So would you believe me if I said it wasn't?"

"No," he admitted.

"You have your own gifts."

"Because I could read that from your reaction?"

"I didn't mean that kind of gift."

He didn't even try for false modesty. He knew she had been as lost in what had occurred as he had been in the endless hours she had made love to him.

Made love. Two people making love.

He acknowledged to himself at least that that was what this had been. He had known her a matter of days. She was as much a mystery as she had been from the first. And he was in love with her.

It wasn't logical or rational or any of the things he needed his world to be. But it was real. And it had been, just as she'd told him, inevitable.

"Ethan?"

He realized that he hadn't answered her last comment. He couldn't even remember what it had been. Not given the realization he'd made, which still had the power to stun him with its force.

"I know you didn't want this to happen," she said.

"It isn't that."

"Then…?"

After this was over. After he'd finished the job he'd been given. There would be time enough to tell her then.

For an instant a feeling of despair, like he hadn't felt since he'd walked into Griff's office at the CIA to tender his resignation, washed over him in a gut-clenching wave. That had been the threat of the loss of his professional life. This…

He wasn't sure what this represented, but as he had done

before, he wrapped his arms around Raine and turned, carrying her with him until they were again lying face-to-face. There was a fine dew of perspiration on her upper lip and her temples. Her mouth was swollen. Well kissed. Well used.

She was his. For the asking. For the taking. She had told him that in every conceivable way she could communicate it to him. All he had to do was accept the gift she'd offered him.

You have your own gifts. And she was by far the most valuable of the ones he'd been given. She had been put into his hands by a man who trusted him to protect her, and, while he did, to also solve the crucial national security case he'd been given.

Another act of trust. One that had been made long before he'd met Raine McAllister. Long before he had fallen in love with her.

There would be time for vows and promises after he had fulfilled the first he had made—a vow of loyalty to a man who had offered him a second chance. Right now...

"We have to make an early start tomorrow."

Her pupils widened slightly, one of those subtle physiological clues he had been trained to look for. He wasn't certain what this one meant. Shock or disappointment or— and his heart ached with the thought—hurt.

Whatever she was feeling, it took her only a second or two to hide her reaction. Her brow cleared, and her eyes again seemed open and transparent, without any trace of disappointment or rebuke.

"Of course," she said. "It's been a very long day."

One that had been full of dangers, both physical and emotional, he'd never expected to encounter. The barriers he'd erected against allowing himself to feel too strongly about anything again had been breeched by the one woman he could never have imagined himself falling in love with. That he had was something he was going to have to come to terms with first before he confessed it to her.

She moved, propping over him on her elbow again. "Shall we say good-night?"

"Don't," he said, unable to bear the brittleness of her tone. "When this is over. There'll be time for this, I promise. Until it is…"

Her eyes changed again as they searched his face. And then she nodded, seeming to accept what he had asked of her. He prayed her gift was powerful enough for her to know that that had truly been a plea for time and not a denial of what she'd offered him.

What she might *not* understand was that this was the biggest risk he had ever taken in his life. And he was willing to take it on the strength of something he would have said less than a week ago he didn't even believe existed.

Chapter Fifteen

"This is Dr. Charles Ellington," Griff said as Ethan and Raine were conducted into his office the following morning. "I believe the two of you may be acquainted."

Ethan walked across the room to offer his hand, which was grasped limply and pumped once. "Dr. Ellington? I'm Ethan Snow. Sorry, but I don't believe we *have* met."

"How do you do?"

Elegantly dressed in a lightweight tropical suit, Ellington looked and sounded like a British colonial official from the last century. His hair, long enough to touch his collar in back, was heavily sprinkled with gray, as were the small, pencil-thin mustache and neat goatee. His dark eyes were a startling contrast to the paleness of his skin.

"I meant that Dr. Ellington may be acquainted with Ms. McAllister," Griff clarified.

"McAllister?" Ellington held out his hand to Raine, who had followed Ethan across the room. "Not Raine? Surely not little Raine?"

Despite the effusiveness of the man's greeting, there was a decided lack of reaction. "I'm very sorry," Raine said. "I'm afraid I don't remember you. Of course, if you knew me when I was 'little Raine,' perhaps that's forgivable."

"Not at all surprising you don't remember, my dear. You

were a child. A very lovely child, who has now become a stunningly beautiful woman. You could hardly be expected to remember all of us."

"All of 'us'?" Raine questioned.

"Who were fortunate to work with you. When Mr. Cabot left his message on my machine last night, he said he was trying to gather information about the CIA's long-ago foray into parapsychology. I called him back as soon as I got home, of course, delighted at the opportunity to reminisce about those days. When I saw you here, I rather naturally assumed you'd been invited for the same reason."

"Ms. McAllister remembers very little from that time, I'm afraid," Griff said.

Ellington glanced at Cabot before he turned back to Raine. "Of course. As I said, she was only a child. An extremely talented one, however."

He took the hand Raine finally offered. Despite Ellington's age and his claim of a long-standing acquaintance, Ethan didn't enjoy watching those long, pale fingers touch her. He controlled the impulse to pull her hand from his by looking at Griff, one brow raised inquiringly.

"Dr. Ellington was one of the psychologists who did testing for the agency during the course of those experiments," Cabot explained.

"A job I achieved almost by default," Ellington said, with a laugh. "They had a hard time finding researchers willing to participate. As a result, they kindly decided to let in a limey who'd done a bit of work for the SAS. Out of the norm compared to what I'd done *there,* but then I'd always been interested in the esoteric."

"You considered those projects to be esoteric?" Ethan asked.

Raine had managed to reclaim her hand, but Ellington was still beaming at her paternally. Ethan wondered if she remembered the Englishman now that she'd had time to study his features and, more tellingly, listen to him talk. With its strong accent and high, almost feminine pitch, his voice was memorable, perhaps even unique in a child's limited experience.

"Oh, for the CIA, certainly," Ellington said. "And I can tell you that many of the old hands weren't happy about the direction the agency was headed. If it hadn't been for Mr. Gardner's support..." Ellington shrugged.

"Why don't we sit down," Griff suggested, "and try to reconstruct as much as you two can remember about those days. My secretary will bring in coffee and iced tea. Or something stronger if you prefer."

The last had clearly been addressed to Ellington. Maybe Griff thought a drink might loosen his tongue or refresh his memory, although neither seemed to be a problem.

Raine had chosen the chair farthest away from the Englishman, leaving Ethan the one between them. Not a bad place to be, he decided, settling into it.

"Whiskey, if you have it. It's bound to be the cocktail hour somewhere within the Empire," Ellington added with a smile.

Griff used the intercom to relay that information to his secretary before he took his seat on the other side of the wide mahogany desk. It didn't take him long to hone in on the opening Ellington had given him.

"Why don't you tell us exactly what you did for the CIA."

"Of course," Ellington said readily. "I was responsible for testing perhaps twenty people. The original number of subjects I was given was somewhat higher, but preliminary screening eliminated most of those. The ones who were left, like little Raine here, for example, were obviously on the up-and-up."

"Meaning they had psychic ability?"

"Some more than others. And some of the talents they exhibited, although impressive, weren't perfectly suited for what the CIA had in mind."

"Which was?" Ethan asked.

"Spying on the Soviets, primarily. You have to remember that satellites were nowhere near as sophisticated then as they are now. In the midst of the so-called Cold War, they were operating primarily from human intel and guesswork. And of course they were terrified the Russians were going to get the jump on us. Rumors abounded that they had psychics who could track troop movements and even the locations of our subs. We wanted someone who could give us the same kind of information about them."

"And were the projects successful in telling the agency what was going on inside the Soviet Union?"

"I have no way of knowing that. All I was privy to were the results of the testing I did."

"Could you tell us about those, then?"

"Normal double-blind validations used to determine how accurate their predictions were. Nothing esoteric there."

"You said that the experiments had Mr. Gardner's support. I take it he wasn't in charge."

"Oh, no. That was Marguery."

"Marguery?"

"James Marguery. Quite the fair-haired boy at the agency in those days. Very bright. Very determined. As I understood it, Grill Flame was his brainchild. Mr. Gardner simply ran interference for it. And let me tell you, there was quite a need for that."

"Who objected?" Griff asked.

Ethan knew Cabot's questions were simply to keep the psychologist talking. Things at the agency hadn't changed enough by Cabot's day that he wouldn't be well aware of who would attempt to quash that kind of experimentation.

"The President for one. He was convinced that if the press found out that the CIA was conducting psychic research, we'd become a laughingstock. Personally I think he was as concerned about the reaction of Congress as with the public."

"Since there was no outcry, I take it the purpose of those projects was never leaked."

"We were all sworn to strict secrecy. National security and all that."

Ellington stopped abruptly as Cabot took a book from the central drawer of his desk and laid it between them. One brow arched, he looked at the psychologist.

"As I was about to say," Ellington went on smoothly, "years later a great deal of information concerning that research was released under the provisions of the Freedom of Information Act. Names of the people involved and much of the outcome had been redacted, as is customary, but the intent of the research was quite clear. There was astonishingly little reaction from the public or the media. Of course, the reputation of the agency had suffered so greatly in the intervening years, I suppose that shouldn't have come as a surprise."

Cabot didn't rise to the bait. He touched the book instead. "And you took the release of that information as permission to break your own oath of silence?"

Ellington's response to that pointed question was a half smile and a slight inclination of his head. "Why not? There's little in my book that hadn't already been made public."

"You claim to have been privy only to the testing of the preliminary subjects and to have no firsthand knowledge of the experiments themselves, so I would guess you used much of the information the CIA released in order to write this.''

For the first time, Ellington looked annoyed. ''Very little, actually. I'd been given a detailed description of the goals of each of the projects so that I could determine which of the subjects I tested might be suitable. Most of what's in the book came from those briefings. I also included methodologies of the preliminary screenings. My insight into the personalities of those in charge. The book is primarily an insider's view of the people who worked on those projects.'' ·

''Such as James Marguery,'' Cabot said. ''Whom you seem to admire very much, by the way.''

Despite having put this meeting together so late last night, again Cabot had done his homework. Ethan felt a scintilla of guilt at the thought of Griff reading Ellington's book into the wee hours of the morning, while he and Raine…

Ethan blocked the image, concentrating instead on the psychologist's answer. If Marguery had been in charge of those experiments—including one code-named Cassandra—then any insight Ellington could give them about him would be important.

''It would be hard to discuss any of this without mentioning Jimmy. He was the heart and soul of those projects. And because they were so sensitive, he never got his due. I tried to remedy that in my book by giving him credit for what he did. I don't believe he ever made DCI, which was certainly his goal. He was Monty's protégé. You might ask him what became of Marguery.''

''Then you haven't heard?'' Griff said.

''Oh, please don't tell me the old man's gone,'' Ellington said, shaking his head with what appeared to be genuine regret. "He was a dominating force in the agency for such a long time."

"Not dead, thank God. He *was* brutally attacked in his home a few nights ago and left in critical condition."

"Attacked? But…why would anyone want to hurt Monty? Or kill him. Is that what you believe? That someone was trying to kill him?"

If the Englishman's surprise wasn't genuine, Ethan thought, he should have been making his living on stage. It would probably have paid more than doing double-blinds for the CIA.

"It would seem that way," Cabot said. "If he weren't such a tough old bird, they would have succeeded."

"But surely Monty's been out of intel for too long to be of interest to anyone. He must be in his eighties by now."

"Mr. Snow and I had visited him the evening he was attacked to inquire about help for an ongoing investigation. Ms. McAllister's name came up at that meeting."

"Then…I take it that since we're both here, you believe the attack on Monty is somehow related to those experiments in parapsychology?"

"It seems to be a possibility," Cabot conceded.

"I can't imagine why. Despite the controversial nature of the projects at the time, they all took place more than a quarter of a century ago. Who would care about them now?"

"You tell us," Ethan suggested.

The dark eyes focused on his face. Ellington's lips pursed as he thought about what he'd been asked.

"Monty, of course. Jimmy Marguery, perhaps. I can't think of anyone else who would even remember what we did after all this time. Maybe some of those like Raine who participated."

"Do you remember any of their names?"

The long white hands lifted in a gesture of dismissal. "I tested only a few of the subjects personally. I only remembered Raine's after you'd introduced us."

"What about other people at the agency who worked on those projects?" Ethan asked. "Do you remember any of their names?"

Looking down at his hands as if he were trying to think, Ellington finally shook his head. "As I said, it's been a very long time ago."

"Any idea where we might find James Marguery?" Cabot asked. "He was no longer with the CIA when I came onboard."

"I expected him to contact me when the book came out. It is, as you say, a very flattering portrait. He didn't, however. And by then we'd lost touch."

"You mention in the book that there's a town in Virginia named for his family."

"Of course. Purportedly they were one of the FFVs."

"FFVs?" Ethan asked.

"First families of Virginia. There was even a plantation, if I remember correctly. Perhaps someone in the area could tell you what's happened to Jimmy."

Cabot made a note on his pad before he looked up again. "There is one small discrepancy that I noticed…. Perhaps there's a simple explanation for it."

"What kind of discrepancy?"

"A project on the CIA's original list of proposals that isn't covered in your book. Something called Cassandra."

There was the smallest hesitation before Ellington answered. "Are you sure? It doesn't ring a bell. Perhaps it was never implemented."

"I'm almost sure it was," Cabot said. "Perhaps it didn't deal with remote viewing."

"Oh, but they all did," Ellington said. "At least the ones

I'm familiar with. Many of them were eventually taken over by the Defence Intelligence Agency. Maybe the DIA can tell you more.''

"Thank you for your time, Dr. Ellington," Cabot said, rising. "You've been most helpful."

"That's all you need, then? You realize we've only scratched the surface of the methodologies employed—"

"This," Cabot interrupted, touching the book on his desk again, "and the information pried loose by the Freedom of Information Act will give us the answers to any other questions that may come up, I'm sure."

"Of course," Ellington said, sounding slightly taken aback to be dismissed so abruptly.

Maybe like so many people of his age, he enjoyed living in the past. Especially if those events were his only connection to history. His only claim to fame.

He rose, stretching across Ethan to offer his hand again to Raine. "So good to see you again, my dear."

"Thank you," she said, ignoring his hand.

After a moment the Englishman straightened. Without any apparent embarrassment over her rejection, he bowed to Raine and then again to Cabot before he walked across the thick carpet to the outer door.

"Perhaps there *is* one other thing you could help us with before you go," Cabot said, stopping him just as he reached out for the knob. "A professional opinion, if you will. As a psychologist. And for a purely hypothetical situation, you understand."

The psychologist's small smile indicated his familiarity with Cabot's disclaimer. "Of course."

"What might cause someone to put himself into a dangerous situation, one he particularly feared?"

Ethan couldn't believe Griff was asking that. Not in front of Raine. He held his tongue, however, recognizing that his surge of fury was the result of the exact emotional involvement Cabot had warned him about last night.

"You'll have to be more specific than that, I'm afraid," Ellington said. "There are so many variables…"

"If someone who had a fear of heights climbed out on the ledge of a building, for example."

If Griff were really interested in a psychologist's opinion, Ethan thought angrily, then he should provide him with all the pertinent information. Otherwise this was nothing more than a farce.

"And what if the person on the ledge has no memory of how he got out there or why he was there."

The dark eyes of the psychologist focused on his face. "That's a particularly interesting scenario. No memory of the event at all?"

"That's right."

Again, Ellington's lips pursed as he considered the situation. "A psychotic episode, perhaps."

"Would you be so kind as to explain exactly what that means?" Cabot asked.

"The ledge seems less dangerous at that moment than something else the person has encountered. Something far more terrifying than their fear of heights had driven them there."

"And yet they don't remember what it was?"

Ellington shrugged. "A form of escape. The human mind is remarkably adept at protecting itself from things it can't or doesn't want to deal with."

"Like repressed memories," the head of the Phoenix clarified.

"Exactly. Something that's painful or frightening in the extreme is repressed or forgotten."

"What about a post-hypnotic suggestion?" Ethan challenged, rejecting the idea that there was anything "psychotic'' about Raine's behavior. "Couldn't that also explain the situation we've described?"

"Perhaps. If this happened during the course of some kind of long-term therapy with the intent of lessening the person's phobia concerning heights, then they *might* be induced to climb out on a ledge. Is that what you're suggesting?"

Ethan realized that his defense of Raine's actions might endanger whatever Cabot had been trying to accomplish. Knowing Griff as he did, he had to trust that his intent was something other than an attempt to embarrass her.

"I'm simply offering another hypothetical solution."

"An interesting theory, but far less likely than the other, I should think," Ellington said, not unkindly.

"Thank you, Dr. Ellington," Griff said, his tone again clearly dismissive.

"You're very welcome. Feel free to call me if you have other questions." He again bowed slightly before he opened the door and stepped through, leaving behind him a thick silence.

"You honestly didn't remember him?"

Griff's question brought Raine's eyes up. She had been looking down on her hands, which rested together in her lap. Her face was controlled, but because they were so attuned after last night, Ethan could tell she was uncomfortable with what had just occurred.

"No more than I remember how I ended up on that ledge."

"And Marguery?"

She shook her head.

"Your contact while working on the project was Mr. Gardner, despite what Ellington indicated about Marguery's role?"

"Actually, I don't remember Mr. Gardner's participation

in the experiments. I remember the maps and the photographs. I remember trying to visualize what was there, but…'' She shook her head again. ''I'm sorry. I'm afraid the rest is a blur.''

There seemed to be nowhere else to go with this. If Raine couldn't remember or if she hadn't known any of the principles involved except Gardner, then they would have to continue to seek other avenues of information.

''Do you want me to check out the place in Virginia that Ellington mentioned?'' he asked Cabot. ''Try to find Marguery?''

''It's a possibility, but I'm afraid we won't find anything there that will do us much good,'' Griff said.

''Meaning?''

''According to Steiner, Jimmy Marguery committed suicide a few years after he left the CIA. Whatever information *he* had about those projects, apparently he took it with him to the grave.''

Chapter Sixteen

"If Marguery's dead, I don't understand why we should come all the way out here."

Although they had had to stop and ask for directions in the nearby town, they were close enough now that Raine could see the house through the trees. The road they'd been directed to had been a winding two-lane threaded between farms that produced the same Tidewater crops they had in the eighteen hundreds: tobacco, sorghum and horses.

"To interview his widow," Ethan said, turning onto the long unpaved drive that led up to Myrtlewood, the Marguerys' plantation house. Evenly spaced, massive oaks stood sentinel on either side of the dirt track, probably planted when the house was built.

Raine had known *who* they were coming to see. What she didn't understand was why Cabot had insisted this interview was necessary or why he thought they should be the ones to conduct it.

Neither he nor Ethan seemed to suspect the old woman was connected to either Cassandra or The Covenant, so the need for Raine's impressions of her shouldn't come into it. Unless there was something going on here she hadn't been told, she didn't see why some other Phoenix operative couldn't have handled this.

"Not all husbands talk to their wives," Raine said. "Especially not that generation. And especially not if their profession involved national security."

"It can't hurt to ask a few questions. Besides, we don't have that many avenues of investigation left."

Famous last words, she thought. Anxiety about this trip had been building since Ethan had told her where they were going, and she had no explanation for what she felt. She didn't argue any further, however, studying the house they were approaching instead.

There was no doubt that in its heyday it had been a show place, clear and tangible evidence of the Marguerys' prominence in the area, a prominence that had caused the town they'd just passed through to be named for them. As they drove nearer, it became increasingly apparent that time had not been kind to the Greek-Revival-style mansion. The columns still gleamed white in the afternoon sunlight, but the plantings around them were wildly overgrown, and the paint was peeling on the front facade.

"Does Mrs. Marguery know we're coming?" Raine asked. She leaned forward to take in the shaded veranda that seemed to stretch around the house.

"We couldn't think of a good reason to give her warning."

And a lot of good ones not to, Raine conceded. Whoever was behind all this had been two steps ahead of them from the beginning.

"Do you know her name?"

With one hand Ethan fumbled a piece of paper out of the inside pocket of his blazer. Without looking at it, he handed it to her.

The lettering was precise, very neat and highly legible. Ethan's, she decided before she concentrated on the information it conveyed.

"Sabina Marguery."

Somewhere within her memory the name struck a chord. Of course, if Marguery had played the central role in the remote viewing projects, she might have met his wife. She had so few clear memories of those days, she couldn't be sure if she had or not.

As Ethan pulled the SUV to a stop in front of the decaying mansion, the anxiety she'd felt since they'd left Washington became full-blown dread. It was all she could do to force her fingers to close around the handle of the car door.

"What's wrong?" Ethan asked as he offered his hand to help her out.

She shook her head. After Ellington's brutal assessment this morning, she was unwilling to admit to anyone what she was feeling. Ethan could ask the questions. All she had to do was to walk into this house and listen.

THE BIG, RAW-BONED WOMAN who answered their knock looked to be in her late forties. Her hair was scraped back and pinned in a tight knot at the top of her head. The face beneath the unbecoming hairstyle was plain, sun-browned and devoid of any softening touch of cosmetics. The brown eyes were as unwelcoming as her clipped answer to Ethan's question had been.

"*I'm* Ms. Marguery," she said. "What do you want?"

"*Sabina* Marguery?"

Ethan had obviously been expecting someone much older, as Raine had. Of course, Marguery wouldn't be the first man to marry a woman years younger than he was.

"Sabina's my aunt. She don't see visitors."

As the woman began to push the door closed, Ethan resorted to the same tactic he'd used the night he'd come to the beach house. "Would you ask her to make an exception? I have some news for her about an old friend."

"And who would that be?" The hostility hadn't lessened, but the forward motion of the door had halted.

"Montgomery Gardner."

"If he's dead, she won't want to know. Says she's outlived everybody else."

"*Not* Mr. Gardner. Would you ask her, please?"

Despite the woman's attitude, Ethan's tone was still relaxed and friendly. As if he had no doubt she would eventually let them in.

He was right. After a moment's hesitation she opened the door enough to let them squeeze through, one at a time. As soon as they had, she closed it again, shutting out the afternoon sunlight.

The hall they had entered was dark and wide and surprisingly cool, despite the outside heat. It took a few seconds for Raine's eyes to adjust to the dimness, but as soon as they had, it was evident that the interior had suffered even more indignities of neglect than had been apparent outside.

The furniture was almost black with age. Given its size, Raine guessed that each piece had probably been custom made for its location, perhaps here on the plantation. The oriental rugs that covered the plank flooring of the long hallway were so faded, or so dirty, Raine amended, taking a closer look, that their patterns were barely distinguishable anymore.

"What was the name?" the other Ms. Marguery asked as she began to lead the way toward the back of the house.

"Ethan Snow and Raine McAllister."

The eyes of Sabina Marguery's niece flicked back to them again, focusing on Raine this time. "I meant the name of her friend you all come to talk about. She's gonna want to know why I'm bringing company in on her."

"Montgomery Gardner," Ethan supplied.

As they moved down the long hall, they passed a narrow staircase that led up to the second floor. If Sabina Marguery was an invalid, she had apparently established a bedroom or sitting room on the ground floor. Far more convenient unless they had a lot of help. And judging from the housekeeping, that didn't seem likely.

"Someone to see you, Sabina," the niece said. She had stopped outside the doorway of a room at the back of the house.

Only one more door was visible at the very end of the hall, which Raine suspected gave access to what would have been the walkway from the main house to the kitchens. The cooking would now be done inside, of course, but at one time it wouldn't have. Not in a wood-framed house like this. It would have been far too dangerous.

Raine heard the murmur of another voice from inside the room, but she couldn't distinguish the words. In response, their reluctant guide added to the information she'd already given.

"They say they have some information about a friend of yours."

Ethan looked unworried, but Raine found herself holding her breath as she awaited Sabina Marguery's decision. Given the strongly negative feelings this meeting had already generated, she wasn't sure she wanted to know any more about James Marguery than she already did.

"You all can go on in," the niece said. "I'll get you some tea. Do her good, too."

With those abrupt instructions, the woman turned and walked across the hall to disappear through a doorway on the opposite side. They watched her exit together, and then Ethan glanced at Raine, eyebrows lifted in disbelief.

"Do you think this is what Cabot had in mind when he sent us?" she whispered.

"I've been working on this for more than six months. If this interview is a dead end, it will simply be the latest of many. Shall we?" He gestured toward the room where their hostess apparently was.

Ethan was right. They were here; they might as well see this through.

Straightening her shoulders, Raine walked through the doorway, uncertain what to expect after the niece's behavior. The first thing she noticed was the smell of cigarette smoke, which seemed to linger over the room like a fog. The next was the woman they had come to see, huddled in an armchair in front of the windows.

Slowly, as her vision adjusted from the darkness of the hall, Raine was able to distinguish Sabina Marguery from her setting. Her eyes, the first thing anyone would ever notice about her, were black and incredibly alive. They were set in a face that seemed relatively unlined, despite her age. The classically pure bone structure was emphasized by the spareness of the flesh that now covered it.

It was obvious she'd been a beauty in her day. Enough of that beauty remained to show through despite the ravages of the long years.

Her head was held at an almost arrogant angle on a long, still-graceful neck. Her hair, pure white, had been twisted into one long braid, which lay over her left shoulder. She wore a black, long-sleeved turtleneck top and black slacks. Her hands were crossed in her lap, the swollen, misshapen bones in their long fingers answering the question of why her niece had answered the door.

"May I help you?"

The English in which the question had been posed was accented. Raine couldn't identify the origin of that accent, but she had heard it before. Not in the same timbre as this voice, perhaps, but with the same intonation. The same slight mispronunciation of the consonants. The elongation of the vowels.

"My name is Ethan Snow. I believe we have a mutual friend in Montgomery Gardner."

Something changed in the patrician face. Or perhaps in the dark eyes. Whatever it was had been instantly controlled. A downward glance toward the brutally damaged hands and then a quick upward tilt of her chin. The thin lips arranged themselves into a smile.

"You know Monty? How delightful. How is he?"

Dying because of something your husband got him involved in.

Raine had no idea where the thought had come from, but for a moment her fury was so great at the injustice that she was afraid she had spoken those words out loud. Only when neither of the other two looked at her did she realize they had only been uttered inside her own head.

"I'm afraid I have some bad news," Ethan said.

"Please don't tell me he's dead. Everyone I know is dead. That is the true curse of old age. Not *this,* as annoying as it is." She held up her hands, the gnarled fingers a contrast to that strangely unlined face.

"He isn't dead, but he was attacked in his home several nights ago. He's still in critical condition."

"How terrible." The tone was right, a mixture of horror and sympathy. "And the police, of course, don't have a clue as to who is responsible."

She hadn't asked them to sit, so that they both were still standing awkwardly before her chair like subjects before the throne of a monarch. It put the old woman in a position of authority, something she seemed determined to maintain. Without waiting for permission, perversely Raine turned and sat down on the faded couch that faced their hostess's chair.

"Actually, they don't. That's why we're attempting to help them," Ethan said before he followed her example.

"We?"

"I work for a private investigative agency called the Phoenix. Mr. Gardner's family has asked us to find out who could possibly want to do him harm. We're following up one of the leads we've uncovered."

"And that's why you've come to *me?* Because you believe *I* may have some information that would help you find out who attacked him? I'm afraid, then, you've had a wasted trip. I haven't seen or heard from Monty in more than twenty-five years."

"We believe the attack had something to do with the Cassandra Project."

The black eyes reacted, but whatever emotion had touched them was quickly controlled. "Cassandra?"

"In Greek mythology she was cursed with the gift of prophecy," Raine said.

For the first time since they'd entered the room, Sabina Marguery looked directly at her. "Cassandra's *curse* was that no one believed her. Hardly the same thing, I should think."

She was right, of course. And with the classical education Monty Gardner's money had paid for, Raine had known that. For some reason, the other had been in her head and then on her tongue.

"This Cassandra was something quite different," Ethan said. "It was a CIA project that we've been told was your husband's brainchild."

The thin lips quirked. "Jimmy had a great number of

those. He was a genius. I can hardly be expected to remember every idea my husband ever had."

Obviously responding to her recognition of the name, Ethan began to embroider on what little they knew about Cassandra. "This was more than just an idea. It was a full-scale research project, something that occupied a great of time and effort."

"He was that kind of man. He threw himself into his work. To his detriment, of course."

"His work, which involved psychic research," Ethan went on. "At the time, that was highly controversial. Your husband must surely have talked to you about—"

"My husband didn't discuss what he did with me. Given the nature of his job, I'm sure you understand."

"Because it involved national security? But surely he didn't distrust you, his own wife." There was just the right touch of skepticism in Ethan's suggestion.

"There were people in the agency who didn't approve of our marriage. Because some of those were in positions of authority over him, Jimmy was careful to avoid giving them cause to dismiss him."

"They didn't approve because you're not an American?" Raine asked.

"I've been a naturalized citizen for many years. I was born, however, in a small village in the Ural Mountains, in a country that has long since disappeared from the map. At the time my husband was with the CIA, any connection with the Soviets, no matter how minor, was looked upon with suspicion."

"So he told you nothing about Cassandra. Or any of the other projects he worked on."

"As I have told you."

Like the accent, the syntax of that phrase was slightly foreign. And like the accent, it was also something Raine had heard before. She just couldn't remember when or where or from whom.

"What about your husband's interest in parapsychology?" Ethan asked. "Did he ever discuss that with you in general terms?"

"My husband was interested in many things. We discussed anything and everything under the sun in the years we spent together, but as I have told you, nothing that ever involved his work. I'm sorry, but I really can't help you. Now if you'll excuse me…"

"Why did you agree to see us?" Raine asked, bringing the black eyes back to her face.

The thin lips moved again, almost a smile. "I don't get many visitors. No one wants to talk to an old woman. I thought you might be entertaining."

The implication was that they hadn't been, but the amusement in her eyes proved that was wrong. She had been highly entertained. And she knew far more about what they had come here to ask than she had told them.

"You didn't like him, did you?" Raine asked.

"Gardner?" There had been no hesitation in her identification. "I barely knew him. Whoever told you he was a friend was mistaken."

"Not even a friend of your husband's?"

"He was my husband's superior. That didn't make them friends."

"Did it make them enemies?"

"Not to my knowledge, but then, I've told you that my husband never discussed his work with me."

"Not even to tell you why he left the agency?" Ethan asked.

"His work there was finished."

"So he told you that much, at least. Just not what that work was."

"Iced tea. Who wants a glass?"

The falsely cheerful question broke the tension that had developed in the room. The big woman who had opened the door to them bustled in bearing a huge tarnished-silver tray loaded with four glasses. The ice in them tinkled pleasantly as she crossed to the table in front of the couch where they were sitting. She bent with a grunt of effort to set the heavy tray on it.

Each of the glasses was dressed with a sprig of mint and had been centered on a linen napkin, folded to cup around the bottom. A bone china plate holding dark, crescent-shaped cookies occupied the center of the tray.

As if they were guests at a tea party, Sabina Marguery's niece handed each of them a napkin and a glass of tea. The third glass was set carefully on the table beside their hostess's chair.

Her misshapen hands never moved from their position in her lap, but her eyes lifted quickly to those of her niece. Whatever communication passed between them resulted in a minute flattening of her lips, as if she were annoyed about something.

Raine wondered if Ethan had caught that interplay. Perhaps he hadn't been watching as closely as she had, using as cover her first sip of tea.

It was surprisingly refreshing, neither too sweet or too strong. Apparently whatever the younger Ms. Marguery's failings as a housekeeper, she was competent in the kitchen.

Neither of them accepted a cookie from the flower-sprigged plate that was offered next. Nor did their hostess, who dismissed them by turning her head.

Her niece put the sweets back on the tray and picked up the final glass of tea. Raine expected her to sit down and join them, but after a slight pause, Sabina Marguery said, "That will do, Elga. Thank you."

"Don't let them tire you out, now, you hear," the other woman said. "You know how you get when you're tired."

The phrase James Marguery's widow used in response was spoken sharply in another language. Apparently it was also convincing. The niece turned with an audible sniff and retraced her path to the door.

"Call me when you want seeing out," she said before she disappeared through it.

There was another tense silence. After a moment Ethan set his untasted tea on the table in front of him.

"Is there anything you can think of that might explain why someone is afraid to have information about the Cassandra Project come to light?"

"I'm sorry about Monty Gardner," their hostess said, "but I can't really help you. I know nothing about any CIA projects."

"Then perhaps you've heard of an organization called The Covenant?"

There was no reaction to Ethan's question, not even that slight widening of the luminous eyes that had betrayed her before. "Should I have?"

"Through your husband, perhaps? Or some of his associates?"

"The name isn't familiar. As I said, that was all a very long time ago. And my memory is not what it once was. Now if you've finished your tea, I shall have to ask you to leave. I must guard my health, I'm afraid. Another inconvenience of age."

In the face of that dismissal, Raine automatically put her glass and napkin on the tray. She glanced toward Ethan, who hadn't moved.

"Do you remember Charles Ellington?" he asked.

"A buffoon. Surely you aren't listening to him."

"We have to. So far he's our only source of information."

"How clever you think you are. Why do you believe I should care if you are stupid enough to listen to an idiot?"

"Because what we are talking about is your husband's legacy. The last important thing he ever did. I should think you'd wish to protect it."

"I have," she said, her eyes very bright.

"Carl Steiner," Raine said, throwing the name into the silence, just as Ethan had used Ellington's. Like her explanation of Cassandra, it had seemed to leap from her mouth before she'd been aware of her intent to say it aloud.

The dark eyes returned once more to her face. "Don't you remember?"

"Remember what?"

That small enigmatic smile lifted the thin lips. "Ask Monty Gardner. He should be able to tell you all you want to know."

"I'm sorry. I thought you understood. Mr. Gardner is in a coma," Ethan said. "He isn't able to tell us anything. We believe that was the intent of the attack against him."

"Then it sounds as if it might be dangerous to talk to you. I choose not to put myself into danger. Not for those people."

Without taking a breath, she raised her voice, calling out for her niece, who must have been waiting in the hall. Listening at the open door?

"Our guests are leaving, Elga. Would you see them out, please? And then bring me my cordial. All this talking has sapped my strength."

The amusement in her eyes this time was almost malicious. All this talking...

"If you'll come with me, please," her watchdog said.

"Your husband—" Raine began, ignoring the prompt.

"Died almost twenty-five years ago," Sabina said. "That's a very long time to be chasing ghosts, don't you think?"

"I suppose that would depend on why one is chasing them."

"But there is really only one reason for that, isn't there. Because one is haunted." As she said the last word, she turned to look at Ethan. "I can't help you, Mr. Snow. Cassandra, if it ever existed, is over and done. Long, long ago. In your case, I think this quest is more a matter of chasing shadows than ghosts. Or tilting at windmills, perhaps. Attacks on the elderly happen all the time in this country. What makes you believe the one on Monty Gardner wasn't simply another senseless urban crime?"

"Because everything that has happened since leads back to Cassandra," Ethan said. "There has to be a connection."

"And you're determined to find it. So much dedication in one so young. Or do you owe a debt of gratitude to Gardner?"

"This isn't about gratitude."

"Not on your part at least." She turned to look at Raine. Challenging.

"Mr. Gardner has been very good to me," she said.

"Monty Gardner *used* you. He took you away from your family because he thought you could give him information he needed. When you couldn't, he got rid of you soon enough, didn't he? Why should you be grateful to him?"

She wanted to say, as she had at the hospital, "Because he's my father." For some reason, the mockery in those dark eyes prevented her from uttering the words.

"Mr. Gardner's treatment of Ms. McAllister isn't in question here," Ethan said. "Someone tried to kill him, and we believe that attempt is connected to Cassandra."

''Then it's really tragic my husband is no longer here to help you. If that project *were* his responsibility, as you claim, then he'd be the only one who could possibly know what that connection is.''

Chapter Seventeen

"I just realized who she reminds me of," Ethan said, glancing at Raine before he inserted the key into the ignition.

She knew he was concerned about how quiet she'd been as they made their way out of the house. There was too much to think about, however. Things had been said that she knew were important, yet she couldn't understand why they should be.

There were also things that had been tantalizingly familiar. When she tried to place them into some kind of context, the connections slid out of her head like quicksilver.

"I'll bite," she said, trying to shake off her sense of disquiet. "Who does she remind you of?"

"Natasha."

He turned to look at her as the engine came to life. Her face must have revealed that she didn't have a clue what he was talking about.

"Boris and Natasha. Rocky and Bullwinkle. Didn't you watch cartoons when you were a kid?"

"I worked for the CIA when I was a kid."

There was a beat of silence.

"Look, maybe—"

"I'm sorry," she said quickly. "That wasn't your fault.

t wasn't anybody's fault. It was just something that happened. I wasn't harmed by it. I don't know why I even said
hat.''

It seemed disloyal to her father. As if she were blaming
him for letting her participate in those experiments. In ac-
uality, she had always considered his agreement to be no
different than any father letting his child serve in the mil-
tary and being proud of their service to their country.

''She was lying through her teeth,'' Ethan said.

''I know. She knows everything that happened. And she
wanted to make it clear to me that she did.''

''Did you recognize the language she spoke to her
niece?''

Raine shook her head. She didn't tell him that it had
sounded familiar, so much so that she knew she should be
able to understand the words. Like those elusive memories,
they had seemed just beyond her grasp.

''Neither did I, but I can tell you it wasn't Russian,''
Ethan said, as he began to back the car into the turn-around
n front of the house.

''Are you sure?''

''The agency runs a very good language school. Not only
was it not Russian, it wasn't any of the old Soviet satellite
anguages they teach there. I know just enough to be able
o recognize most of those. *That* was something I've never
heard before.''

Raine knew that she had. Just as she knew she had heard
the idioms sprinkled through the old woman's English. She
had encountered both at some time in the past, but since
she couldn't remember when or where, that certainty was
no help at all in solving the mystery Sabina Marguery represented.

Ethan had turned the car so that it was pointing back
down the drive. He didn't seem inclined to leave, however.

Maybe, as she was, he was still caught up in the web of lies and deceit the old woman had woven.

"Someone who knew a lot about how things operate in Washington told us that The Covenant was the reincarnation, or maybe the continuation, of an older society," he said. "One that's been around since the founding of this country."

"I don't understand. What does that have to do with what she said?"

"If Marguery's family really was what Ellington claimed, maybe there's a link."

The psychologist had said the Marguerys were one of the founding families of Virginia. The mansion, even in its state of decay, gave testimony to their wealth and power during the period during which it had been constructed.

"A link to that other society?" she asked.

"Your father compared The Covenant to the Hell Fire Club, but I doubt that would be the prototype for an organization bent on politicizing morality."

"What would be? The Illuminati? The Masons? The Knights Templar?" She laughed, mocking the ridiculousness of her suggestions, especially the last. When she glanced at Ethan's face, she realized that his lips hadn't moved in response. "Strike that one," she said, her inclination to laugh disappearing as she remembered that group's history. "I think they were all burned at the stake for heresy."

"And for treason against the crown," Ethan added softly.

Traitors. After all, that was what this was about. People in positions of authority working against the well-being of their country.

Ethan had turned to look at her, his eyes silver in the late-afternoon light. He had told her last night that while the investigation was ongoing, their being lovers could be distracting.

It was certainly proving to be for her. Everything about him. The shape of his mouth. How it felt moving against her body. A jolt of pure sexual reaction ran through her veins, reminding her of how much she had loved the feel of his arms around her.

She had also cherished what they'd shared today. Working together. Brainstorming possibilities.

The perfect emotional complement to the physical unity they had discovered last night. An intimacy so in tune, it had sometimes seemed as if *he* could read *her* thoughts.

"It doesn't matter about the origins of The Covenant," he said. "It only matters that we figure out why they're so afraid of what we might discover about Cassandra."

"She was right, you know. It was the fact that no one believed what she said that was Cassandra's curse. She knew what would happen, but no one would listen to her. And she was forced to watch all of them die."

His attention had refocused on the driveway, but something about her tone caused him to turn back to her, his eyes questioning. "Forced to watch who die?"

"Everyone she ever loved." As she whispered the words, she shivered.

"Raine…"

"I need to see him, Ethan. I need to see him this afternoon. Especially after listening to that…God, I don't even know what to call her." She shivered again, rubbing her hands over her arms.

"Don't call her anything," he said as he reached down to shift into drive. "Don't even think about her."

She nodded, relieved they were finally leaving Myrtlewood. As the SUV began to pick up speed, she fastened her seat belt and then stole a glance at his profile.

Through the driver's side window, she noticed a grove of trees about a hundred yards to the left of the drive. The sense of familiarity she'd felt in the parlor nagged at the edges of her memory.

As far as she could remember, she'd never before been here. And yet she knew that if she walked under the low-hanging branches of those ancient oaks, she would find something she'd seen before. Something important not only to understanding who she was, but what was going on.

"Those trees…" she began, and then realized she didn't know anything else to tell him.

Ethan turned to look at her, and then, following the direction of her gaze, out his window. "Those oaks? Did you see something?"

She hadn't. Not in the sense he meant. Nothing real. Nothing tangible.

What she'd felt was a compulsion as strong—and possibly as dangerous—as the one she had followed the night of The Covenant's fund-raiser. The one that had eventually led her onto that ledge.

"Stop the car."

"What is it?"

"Just stop the car," she said again.

She turned her head, looking back at the grove they had passed. The Mercedes began to slow as Ethan directed it onto the shoulder of the drive.

"What's back there?" he asked. He killed the engine and then looked over his shoulder at the trees.

Without answering him, Raine wrapped her fingers around the handle of the door. After a second's hesitation, she lifted, opening it. The sound made him turn back to her, but by then she was already climbing out of the car.

She stood outside in the twilight stillness. Despite the fact that they were far from the noises of civilization, there were none of the normal sounds of insects or birds. The silence that surrounded her was both eerie and complete.

Ethan had gotten out of the car and walked around it to stand beside her. She had been unaware of either movement, too attuned to the sensations that begun bombarding her.

"What is it?"

"I don't know. Something…"

Unable to articulate any further what she was feeling, she began to walk toward the grove of trees. She was aware, on some level at least, that Ethan trailed her, but it was as if she had developed tunnel vision. Only the darkness that gathered under the oaks interested her now.

"Raine?"

She didn't even consider answering, walking with a single-minded determination across the uneven ground. And he didn't call to her again.

As she neared the edge of the trees, the unnatural stillness she had noticed before seemed to deepen. Despite the heat that had held steady throughout the day, there was a definite drop in temperature.

That might be explained by the lateness of the hour or by the thickness of the shade, but in her heart she knew it had less to do with the weather conditions than with this location. What she felt as she entered the grove was the kind of spectral cold that chilled to the marrow of the bone.

The canopy formed by the oaks was high, cutting off sunlight that would have encouraged undergrowth. There was nothing to hamper her passage between their thick trunks. No brush. No fern. Nothing but the rich, black loam of the ancient forest floor.

There was no other smell like this. Earthy, almost fetid, it suggested a primordial world untouched by man's contamination.

She knew instinctively that she was approaching the center of the grove. And she knew—as she realized she had from the first—what she would find there.

She cleared a small rise in the ground, and the pond of her visions lay in front of her, looking exactly as she had seen it. Once in her studio the night Ethan had arrived and once more when she had bent to put her lips against her father's forehead.

Light from the setting sun slanted across its surface, tinting the water red. Her steps faltered, as if her body were physically reluctant to make the final approach.

Ethan caught up with her, taking her arm. The touch of his hand was comforting in the face of the confrontation with something she had recognized from the first as inherently evil.

"What is it?" he asked.

She shook her head, unsure even now of the pond's significance. Despite the eerie cold, despite the blood-red surface, it managed to appear serene and tranquil in the late-afternoon stillness.

Ethan's hand seemed to urge her forward. Fighting an inclination to turn and run, she obeyed. As they neared the edge of the dark water, there was a roaring in her ears. The same sense of disorientation she'd felt in the parlor at Myrtlewood returned, making her light-headed.

"You've been here before," Ethan said.

Given that she'd led him here from the road, a vantage point from which the pond could not be seen, that was obvious. Clearly, she had known it was here, but she had no idea how.

"A long time ago."

As she said the words, she knew they were true. She had been a child. She had stood behind one of the oaks, looking toward the pond, and she had seen—

She couldn't remember. Something that had branded this image on her consciousness so that she had never forgotten it.

"Raine?"

"Something happened here. Something…" She hesitated, because she had used the word before in a different context, but it was the only one that was appropriate. "Something unspeakable. Something I wasn't supposed to see."

Again, although she hadn't known all of that when she began the sentence, she knew it now. Something had been done here that no one was supposed to have witnessed. And she had.

"You can't remember what you saw?"

She tried, struggling against the restraints of a memory long repressed. Deliberately repressed? Because what it contained was too painful to deal with?

Apparently it still was. She shook her head again, pulling her gaze away from the crimsoned surface to look up at his face.

"I wasn't supposed to see it, and now I'm not supposed to remember."

"But you *do* remember something."

"I kept seeing this. The pond with the rays of the setting sun across it. The night you came to my house. And when I was with my father in the ICU. I saw it, and I knew it was important, but I don't know why."

"Obviously something connected to Marguery and Cassandra."

That was the thread that joined everything. Whatever Cassandra had been, it was still powerful enough to haunt her after all these years. She shivered, conscious once more of the chill that surrounded the grove.

She couldn't tell Ethan any more than she already had.

Something had happened here. She had seen it, and then she had blocked it from her memory. Just as Ellington had suggested.

"I don't know. I don't remember. I don't *want* to remember. Not even now."

"Then let's get out of here," Ethan suggested.

There was no reason not to, she realized. She was no closer to an answer than she had been in her studio that first night.

He took her arm, turning her in the direction of the car. As soon as the pond was out of her sight, she realized that she remembered more about this place than its location. She started forward, walking away from the SUV, drawing Ethan with her.

"What is it?" he asked again.

Despite the fact that she didn't answer, he followed her through the overgrown grass until they encountered a worn path. At the end of it, atop a gently sloping hill, lay a shaded cemetery surrounded by a low, wrought-iron fence. An ornate *M* had been fashioned from the same metal and attached to the gate that guarded it.

Thick with rust, it still swung open at the touch of her fingers. She hesitated, but Ethan's hand around her arm represented enough security that she was able to step through the gate and into the graveyard.

The roughly hewn headstones were covered with lichen, making the inscriptions difficult to read. A few of the dates could be deciphered, in spite of the fading light. Tracking them, she could also track the development of the cemetery itself.

The oldest graves were from the 1700s. Green with age and worn by the elements, their markers bore the names of the earliest members of the Marguery line, whose given names were repeated through the generations.

She hadn't been aware when she'd entered the gate of what had sent her here. As she wandered among the stones, increasingly agitated, her eyes sought the one name that seemed to be missing.

"Raine?" Ethan again. Still concerned. "What is it? What are you looking for?"

Not what, but who. This was what she'd been seeking when she left the car. This is what had drawn her. The pond and this.

"For Marguery."

There was a long hesitation before Ethan offered the obvious. "They're *all* Marguerys."

All the Marguerys. Except the one who should be here.

"*He* isn't here," Raine said.

The husband of the woman who still lived at Myrtlewood, the man Sabina and Charles Ellington had both told them died more than twenty-five years ago, the heir to the name and the plantation, was not buried in its cemetery.

Chapter Eighteen

"I'm not sure what it means," Ethan said into his cell phone, "but I thought you should know."

Ethan, seated behind the wheel of the SUV, listened to Cabot's response. As he did, his eyes found Raine's, and again she could read the depth of his concern for her within them.

"Griff wants to know why you think that's so important," he said.

"Because he *should* be there. He's a Marguery. Either he was buried somewhere else, against family tradition…or he isn't dead."

She didn't want to talk about this. She didn't want to even *think* about the possibility Marguery could be alive. Most of all, she didn't want to be on the grounds of Myrtlewood another second.

Ethan relayed the information, and then he added, "Marguery's widow knows far more than she was willing to share. Can you get any information about their relationship? And about her background. She says she was born in a country in the Ural Mountains that's since disappeared. I couldn't place the language she spoke to her niece, but it wasn't Russian. Oh, and the niece might be another avenue of inquiry. Elga Marguery. Late forties, early fifties. She seems to have assumed a caregiver role for the old woman.''

The silence as he listened stretched longer this time. At the end of it, he said, ''Let me know what you find.''

He broke the connection and then laid the phone on the center console. ''Maybe we should just go back to the house and ask. There could be a simple explanation for Marguery not being buried there.''

''No.''

''Why not?''

It was a legitimate question for which Raine had several answers. None of which she was going to share with him. *Because I've always been afraid of the dark. Because that fragile old woman scares me to death. Because I need desperately to get away from this place.*

''She won't be any more forthcoming than she was before,'' she said instead.

''It would be hard for her to prevaricate about where her husband's buried. Whatever she says could be checked.''

That wasn't really the problem. Not as far as Raine was concerned. The problem was her absolute conviction that if James Marguery were dead, he would have been interred in the family plot with all his ancestors. The fact that he wasn't—

''She'd lie, even if telling the truth would serve her better.''

She knew what she'd just said was true, but she couldn't tell him how she knew. Any more than she could explain why the thought that James Marguery might be alive was so terrifying to her.

It was as if things she had once known and then forgotten were slowly coming back. The memories were clouded by the passage of time or by her own efforts to forget them, but they were beginning to seep back into her brain. And she didn't want them there.

"You mean Sabina?"

Ethan seemed puzzled by her vehemence. She could no more explain her hostility to the old woman than she could her certainty that she should have recognized the language Sabina had spoken to her niece.

"Nothing she told us was true. What's the point in giving her another opportunity to lie?"

Before she completed the sentence, a black car turned off the deserted two-lane and started down the long driveway to the house. As if mesmerized, they watched its approach.

It was a late-model town car, its dark paint mirrorlike in the twilight. Both the size and quality seemed almost out of place in this rustic setting.

Whether it was her sudden realization of how out of place it was or whether the abilities that had failed her so many times since she'd come to Washington had finally returned, she knew, with as much surety as she had ever known anything in her entire life, that whoever was in that car meant them harm. Having slowed to make the turn into the driveway, the automobile was again gathering speed. A plume of dust followed as it barreled recklessly down the dirt track.

"We have to get out of here," she said.

"What the hell are you talking about?"

The tinted window on the passenger side of the Lincoln began to lower.

"That car. There's someone—"

Her warning was cut off as Ethan pulled her down. He threw his body over hers, pressing her ribs into the hard console between them.

Her automatic yelp of surprise was buried under the hail

of bullets that slammed into the body of the M-Class, shattering windows. Small, round pellets of the broken safety glass rained down over her.

"Stay put," Ethan ordered, turning the key he'd already inserted in the ignition.

The engine roared to life. He floored the accelerator, sending the SUV off the shoulder and back onto the drive. The back tires fishtailed as they encountered its mix of dirt and loose chert.

As Ethan fought to regain control of the Mercedes, she raised her head enough to see out the back window. The car that had sped by seconds before was coming out of a deep turn that would bring it back around.

Although the driver's side window was facing her, it was too darkly tinted to even venture a guess as to how many people were in the vehicle, much less attempt identification of any of them. She glanced back toward the front windshield in time to see Ethan wrestle the M-Class into alignment with the drive.

Despite the skid, he had apparently never taken his foot off the gas. The big SUV seemed to leap forward, headed toward the blacktop at the end of the drive. When Raine looked out the back window again, she saw that at least the town car wasn't closing the gap between them.

Ethan hardly slowed when he reached the turn, the vehicle making its entrance onto the highway on two wheels. The Mercedes regained its footing instantly and then surged forward again. As it did, a squeal of tires came from behind them as their pursuers attempted the same maneuver.

"Fasten your seat belt," Ethan ordered without looking at her.

"Are you going to try to outrun them?" she asked as she pulled the shoulder strap across her body and slipped the buckle into the lock.

''Unless you've got something comparable to whatever they just used. An assault rifle, maybe.''

She leaned across the console, reaching for the buckle of his belt as he attempted to pull the strap across his chest with one hand. She slipped it into the slot, as he raised his eyes to the rearview mirror. Whatever he saw caused his lips to tighten.

''*Can* you outrun them?'' she asked.

''We're about to find out.''

The winding two-lane that had appeared so scenic on their journey to the plantation now seemed like something on the European racing circuit. Ethan's total concentration was required for navigating the SUV through its hairpin turns.

Only on the few straightaways did either of them dare look back, he by employing the rearview mirror and she by glancing over her shoulder. Although the black car didn't appear to be gaining, neither were they able to increase the distance between them. And whoever was driving didn't seem inclined to give up the chase.

''Here.''

She turned to find Ethan, his eyes still on the curving road, holding his phone out to her. She took it quickly, allowing him to return both hands to the wheel.

''Cabot?''

''There isn't time. Dial 911. Let's see if we can get the locals to make them back off.''

Considering the damage the semiautomatic had done to the SUV, they wouldn't have any trouble convincing the police of the threat. And she doubted that whoever was in the town car would want to explain to the cops.

As she dialed, Ethan told her as much about their location as he could. She relayed it to the dispatcher, who sounded incredibly blasé as she took the information down.

Maybe the crime rate around here was higher than she'd imagined, Raine decided as she pressed the off button on the cell.

Unable to resist, she glanced back again. The black car was closer than it had been before. With a higher center of gravity to worry about, Ethan was having to ease the SUV through the curves more carefully than the other driver.

"Hold on."

Despite Ethan's warning, she was thrown against the door as he put the M-Class into another of those hairpin turns. As the road began to straighten, from somewhere in the distance came the wail of a siren.

"That was quick," Ethan said.

She glanced back at the town car, which was just coming out of the curve. Either they hadn't yet heard the sound of the approaching police cruiser or they hadn't realized its significance. She continued to watch, expecting at any moment to see the driver execute another of the skidding turn-arounds he'd made back at the plantation.

"Son of a bitch."

Ethan's expletive was soft, but so obviously heartfelt that it pulled her eyes back to the front windshield. At the end of the straightaway, two police cars had been pulled up nose-to-nose, so that they blocked both lanes of the county road. Judging by their color and markings, the cars were local law enforcement and not state.

Raine's first thought was that they'd certainly gotten the roadblock quickly organized. Then, with the sudden realization of how impossible the timing of it was, she understood why Ethan wasn't slowing. He had obviously come to that same conclusion before she had.

"Hold on," he ordered again.

She put her hands on either side of the seat, trying to

brace herself. Her eyes considered the terrain on both sides of the narrow two-lane the cops had blocked.

As she did, she realized that whoever had set this up knew exactly what they were doing. Even in the dim light of dusk, she could see the ditch that ran along the right-hand side of the road. A stand of pines guarded the left. And they were approaching both of them far too fast.

"Ethan."

She only had time to say his name before the SUV veered off the pavement to the left, seemingly headed toward the first stand of trees. It felt as if they'd become airborne as they jolted over the shoulder and then plowed onto the grassy verge. Raine fought the urge to close her eyes as Ethan guided the car around the trunk of one of the pines.

On some level she was aware that the cops who'd set up the barricade were shouting. She couldn't tell if the words, unintelligible at this distance, were directed at them or at one another.

Her attention was so tightly focused on the trees Ethan was trying to maneuver between that she didn't have room in her head right now for any other consideration. Ethan's hands shifted on the wheel as he struggled to guide the Mercedes around the pines, which appeared in front of their headlights with the speed and regularity of targets on some incredibly challenging video game.

Then, like a miracle, just ahead of them was a narrow opening between two of the trees. Although it would be close, the gap seemed wide enough to allow them to shoot through and get back up onto the highway at a point past the police cruisers. Only a couple more of the pines to steer around—

There was no way Ethan could have foreseen what the roadside vegetation, thickly overgrown with the spring rains, was hiding. The right wheel of the SUV jolted into the ditch that had been camouflaged by the tall grass.

With the speed at which they had been traveling, the vehicle didn't come to a stop. The sudden loss of traction was enough to turn it, sending it sideways through the trees around which Ethan had, up until now, been successfully navigating.

He struggled to turn the wheel into the skid, trying to regain control. Instead, Raine watched in horror as one of the trees grew larger and larger in the frame of her shattered window.

There was no time to brace herself before the passenger side of the Mercedes slammed into the massive trunk, instantly throwing her world into an encompassing darkness.

Chapter Nineteen

"Time to wake up."

The first thing Raine became aware of was pain. A dull throbbing in her head, which seemed to correspond to the beating of her heart. It took a moment to decide it was bearable. Another to know it wasn't life threatening.

Whoever had spoken—and she wasn't certain if it had been a man or a woman—put a hand under her elbow, applying an upward pressure. Too disoriented to think about resisting and only with that help, she managed to get to her feet, an effort that caused the ache in her head to intensify.

During the awkward process she had discovered that her wrists had been tied together behind her back. Whatever material they were bound with bit into her flesh so tightly that her fingers had gone numb.

Pressure against the movement of her lashes and the solidness of the darkness that surrounded her verified that she had also been blindfolded. She swallowed the bile that climbed into her throat, trying desperately to hold on to her flagging courage. Like the idea that James Marguery might be alive, having her eyes covered terrified her to an extent that seemed disproportionate to the act.

The most important thing was that she was still alive,

she told herself. And right now, that seemed cause for celebration.

Despite her attempt to focus on the positive, she knew her survival might be short-lived. They had already tried to get rid of her once by getting her out onto the ledge at the hotel. Twice, she amended, remembering that rain of bullets. She couldn't imagine what had prevented them from completing the job now that she was totally in their control.

Staggering slightly, either from the effects of the blow to her head or from the stiffness that had resulted from the awkward position she'd been lying in, she could do little but follow the guidance of the hand on her arm. As she did, she tried to gain some control over her fear by concentrating on her surroundings.

There was no noise but the sound of their footsteps, echoing off wooden floors. Which meant that they were no longer outside, she realized belatedly.

At the same time she became aware of the same pervasive smells that had surrounded her this afternoon. Mold. Decay. Dust. The distinctive aromas of an old house, badly in need of care.

Myrtlewood.

Terror welled up in her chest. She made herself take a calming breath and then another, until she could once more establish the familiar pattern of breathing.

Just as she was beginning to overcome that blind panic, the toe of her shoe caught on something, sending her stumbling forward. She was prevented from falling only by the hand that had tightened around her arm.

As soon as she recovered her balance, she realized that the surface underfoot was softer now and their footsteps no longer echoed. Had she tripped over the ancient rug that centered the main hall, its colors obliterated by age and dirt? If so, that meant her guide was taking her to see the old woman. Marguery's widow.

Except if Marguery wasn't dead—

Her guide came to an abrupt halt. There was a slight creak directly in front of her. She tried to remember if the hinges of the parlor door had made that noise this afternoon when Sabina's niece had escorted them through it.

Before she could decide, the grip around her arm tightened, urging her forward again. Despite her attempts to orient herself, she didn't know for sure where she was or who might be in the room into which she was being led. No way to know if she was again about to be taken to some dangerous height and deserted.

"In the chair, if you please."

There was no mistaking the arrogant tone of command. It had haunted her nightmares for decades. Dreams she could never remember but which left her drenched with sweat and trembling.

Hearing it now, her blood froze. Then her heart began to pound, sending it racing through her veins again, driven by an adrenaline rush so powerful it made her dizzy.

Trying to control the flood of memory James Marguery's voice evoked, she had allowed herself to be drawn farther into the room. After a few feet she was roughly pushed down into a straight-back wooden chair.

"It's so good to see you again, my dear."

She couldn't have answered him if her life depended on it. Maybe it did, she admitted, but her throat was too constricted to speak, aching with tears she refused to let him see her shed.

"Surely it's been too long to hold a grudge," Marguery prompted when she didn't respond.

The old woman cackled, her laughter another sound

Raine now remembered. Like nails dragged across a chalkboard, it set every nerve on edge.

She licked dry lips, determined not to give in to her terror. After all, she was no longer five years old and afraid of the dark.

Or of bogymen. No matter how real they were.

"Where's Ethan?" The silence that followed her question frightened her almost as much as the rest.

They want you to think the worst, she told herself. They're deliberately trying to frighten you. She wondered if they had any idea how well they were succeeding.

"Mr. Snow is enjoying our hospitality in another location. He won't disturb us, I promise you."

The last sentence had been touched with amusement. She examined the words of the first, trying to decide if she dared trust that was true.

Of course, she had never before been able to depend on anything he or Sabina told her. And if she couldn't believe Marguery, there was only one way to determine if Ethan was alive.

She closed her mind to everything in the room, reaching beyond it. Probing an unknown darkness. Searching it. After years spent denying her gift, she called on every shred of her ability.

Only after she had almost given up hope did she find what she was looking for. Somewhere, not far from here, she could sense him. Ethan was alive, but she knew from what she felt that something was wrong. Had he been injured in the accident?

There was nothing she could do to help, even if he were, and so she closed her mind, blocking out that concern. Worrying about Ethan would only weaken her. She knew she would need all her strength to deal with the two people before her.

Making the most difficult decision of her life, she deliberately broke the connection to Ethan. It was enough to know he was alive. It *had* to be enough.

She needed to concentrate on the man in *this* room. A man who was supposed to have died twenty-five years ago.

"Satisfied?"

She ignored Sabina's mocking question. "What do you want?"

They had always wanted something. And she had always given them whatever they demanded.

She had been a child then, unable to resist. She was a child no longer.

"As you can imagine, Raine, you have caused us a *great* deal of trouble."

She *could* imagine. All their attempts to get rid of her. To prevent what she knew from ever coming out. If only they had known how little she'd remembered.

Now it was to her advantage that they didn't know she'd blocked those memories. It had been the only way she could survive them. That and the support of Monty Gardner.

"That doesn't tell me what you want," she said.

Her voice seemed remarkably steady. Especially since, now that the dam had been breeched, the memories she had denied for decades were flooding her consciousness.

"It's really very simple. We need to know what you've told them."

"*Exactly* what you told the Phoenix," Sabina added.

Marguery's Igor. His alter ego. Not that he'd ever had need of another.

"Why don't you read my mind?" Raine suggested, echoing the old woman's mockery of this afternoon.

"Don't be impertinent, my dear," Marguery warned softly. "It doesn't become you."

He sounded like a headmaster, threatening some recalcitrant pupil. And no matter what happened, that was a role she had no intention of playing. Never again. It had taken her too long to put these particular demons behind her.

Her life and Ethan's might depend on how well she would be able to handle their questions. If she told them the truth—that she had revealed nothing about Cassandra because she had remembered nothing—they certainly wouldn't hesitate to dispose of her. Just as they had tried to dispose of the only other person who knew the full story of their treachery. And if she claimed to have already provided the authorities with the information, they would have no reason to keep her around.

It was a lose-lose situation. It might be convenient for Marguery to know what Cabot and the authorities knew, but it wasn't essential. Their questioning wasn't intended to solicit information so much as to demonstrate once again their power over her.

It was the kind of intimidation they enjoyed most. With the help of Mr. Gardner, she had managed to escape once. That she was again under their control must seem like poetic justice.

Maybe they would enjoy it enough to prolong the interrogation, although she wasn't sure what value there might be in that. Cabot knew where they were. Would he become concerned if Ethan didn't eventually check in? And if so, how long would it take him?

"We're waiting, my dear."

"If you're waiting on me to tell you anything, I should probably warn you to get comfortable. It's going to be a while."

There was a small silence.

"It's seems our little darling has grown rebellious," Marguery said.

It was the same tone he had used to such effect in the past. She steeled herself against its sarcasm, which had once bothered her almost as much as the physical punishments he'd meted out.

"She's just not 'your little darling' any longer."

She sensed rather than heard movement. Before she had time to wonder what it meant, the back of his hand exploded against her cheek, splitting her lip. The shock of being struck blindly, unexpectedly, was worse than the pain.

For a moment she became that child again, cowering before his displeasure. Then anger replaced those hard-learned lessons of fear and humiliation.

"She isn't *anything* that belongs to you anymore," she said defiantly.

That had been Monty Gardner's gift. He had taken her away from her aunt and uncle and provided her with the only stability she'd ever known, even though he had been forced to destroy her identity to do so. If he had kept her with him, he had feared that eventually they would find her. So he had given her his grandmother's name and then had hidden her among hundreds of other girls her age.

Even after Marguery's suicide, mistrustful of Sabina's intentions, Gardner had kept her hidden. She had grown content in her new life, one that was, for the first time in her memory, without threat or intimidation.

From his kindness had been born her wish that Mr. Gardner could be her father. She had thought of him as her protector for so long that eventually desire became her reality. Although at some point she had known it was fantasy, the leap to thinking of him as her father had been seamless.

Now once again face-to-face with her real family, she had been forced to recognize that the bond she had so desperately wanted, so desperately needed, wasn't true. The life she had created for herself was based on a tissue of lies. With the reappearance of her uncle, it was tumbling down around her like a house built of cards.

Not *all* lies. Not all. She clung like a lifeline to the testimonials in the file Cabot had shown her.

And to the tenderness of a good man. A man who had loved her with both gentleness and respect. A man who believed that she, too, was a good person.

"It will be far easier if you tell us what we want to know," her uncle said. "You will in the end, you know."

He sounded so certain. And why shouldn't he be. He had always been able to make her do what he wanted. Even when she tried to resist, he had always worn her down.

"Not this time," she promised.

She had nothing with which to defend herself but her will. Against an enemy who knew all the ways to break it.

EVENTUALLY THEY WOULD send someone out here to check on him, Ethan told himself again. All he had to do was be patient. And not think about the glimpse he'd gotten of Raine, lying unconscious on the back seat of the other police car.

Under the directions of that bastard Ellington, the sheriff and his deputy had manhandled him past the cruiser, using their nightsticks in ways that had made his struggle to get to her not only useless but costly. And incredibly painful.

The image of her face, colorless except for the bruise on her temple, had haunted him since they'd dragged him to the root cellar and pushed him down the short flight of steps. He'd been semiconscious by then, but the sound of the trap door slamming over his head had created a sense of despair so deep it had maddened him. Despite what he now believed to be a broken collarbone and a couple of cracked ribs, he had assaulted the boards, pounding on them with the fury he wanted to expend against the sheriff and his deputy.

They had ignored everything he'd tried to tell them, deferring to the prissy Englishman. Sabina had called him a buffoon, but obviously he was her buffoon.

The niece had probably been instructed to phone him when she'd gone back to the kitchen. That's what she'd communicated to Sabina when she'd handed her the tea.

Ellington had then set up the roadblock, using the locals who were apparently used to taking their orders from the old woman. The last link to the powerful family who had lived in this county for more than two hundred years.

He didn't know what story Ellington had told them. Maybe that he and Raine had stolen something from the house. That didn't explain why they would agree to bring them back to Myrtlewood rather than arrest them, however.

Despite his anger that the sheriff had bought in to whatever lies he and the old woman had concocted, Ethan acknowledged that the reason he was still alive was undoubtedly the presence of him and his deputy. As soon as they left…

The image of Raine lying injured and helpless flashed through his consciousness again. He should have done something—*anything*—rather than let those bastards separate them. He should have kept fighting. He should have made them beat him to death right there by the cruiser.

And what good would that have done Raine?

That realization, combined with the locals' willingness to use their sticks, had convinced him to stay alive, even if that meant their being separated. He was still functional and eventually someone would open that damned door. With the element of surprise on his side, he might have a chance.

To keep from losing his mind while he waited, he began

again to run his hands around the perimeter of his prison. He had already explored its features as well as he could, given the pitch darkness, but doing it once more was far better than wondering what was happening to Raine.

Think, he urged himself. *Outside* the box they've put you in. Griff had always told them that if they came to a wall they couldn't go over, they had to find a way around. Despite trying to do exactly that during the endless minutes he'd spent in this hellhole, he hadn't discovered one.

He hunched his aching shoulder in an attempt to ease the pain of splintered bones, but it didn't seem to help. He leaned forward, putting his forehead against the stone wall. He closed his eyes in despair, despite the blackness that surrounded him.

And then, too disheartened to pray, he finally heard the sound he'd been waiting for. Someone was coming down the walk that led from the back of the decaying mansion to the root cellar.

He pushed away from the wall and listened. The footsteps were definitely headed his way. He could tell nothing about them other than their direction. Not even if they belonged to a man or a woman.

Moving as soundlessly as he could, he sprinted across the room, stooping at the side of the steps that led up to the slanting trap door. If they lifted it, there was no way in hell they were going to get it closed again with him inside.

His heart in his throat, he listened as the bolt was drawn out of its slot. *Marguery? Or the cops?*

It made no difference, he thought as the powerful muscles in his thighs tensed in preparation. As soon as the door began to lift, he would charge up those steps, get his shoulders under it, and throw it open. He didn't allow himself to think about what that would do to the damaged collarbone, which would have to bear part of its weight.

The sound of the door being lifted was accompanied by a widening rim of lesser darkness that outlined the opening. It took him a moment to identify the other sound that filtered in with the moonlight as the drumming of a hard rain.

He forced himself to wait a second or two, adrenaline roaring through his body, dulling the pain. Making him forget everything but the possibility of escape and of getting to Raine.

The opening continued to widen, and then whoever was up there directed the beam of a flashlight into the cellar. As it began a slow sweep across the dirt floor, he knew he couldn't afford to wait any longer.

Now.

He put his palm flat on one of the steps and vaulted onto the stairs. He clambered up them, getting his shoulders under the door just as he'd planned.

He strained upward, jerking it out of the hands of the person at the top and throwing it wide open. Whoever had been holding it stumbled backward, shocked into dropping the flashlight.

Ethan was aware of it rolling away from them, but he was more concerned about what its light had revealed in the seconds before it hit the ground. For an instant, framed against the night sky, had been an amorphously shaped creature. Ethan immediately identified the long dark object it held as a weapon. He latched onto that with both hands, wrenching it away.

As soon as he had control of what he now had discovered was a shotgun, he brought the weapon around in a vicious arc. The stock connected with the side of his victim's head with a hollow thud, felling him.

Panting from his exertions, Ethan reversed the weapon and stood over the fallen body, watching for any movement that would indicate consciousness. The rain pounded down, running out of his hair and down into his eyes.

When his quarry offered no sign of resistance, Ethan scrubbed his forearm across his face to clear his vision. When he could see again, he realized that the person he'd downed had appeared to be shapeless because they'd been wearing a plastic poncho.

He straightened slowly, keeping the shotgun still pointed downward. The adrenaline was fading, its loss leaving him exhausted and in pain.

But alive, he reminded himself.

He stepped over whoever he'd knocked out to pick up the flashlight. He directed it at the flaccid face that was half hidden by the hood of the raincoat and recognized Elga Marguery. Sabina's niece.

She had either been sent to bring him into the house or, more likely, to finish him off. Which meant the sheriff must be gone.

That left the old woman and Ellington inside. Unless there had been someone else in the black car this afternoon. It wouldn't be impossible to drive and shoot that kind of high-powered weapon at the same time, but he believed the accuracy of the gunfire argued against it.

He had to plan as if there were three of them. Better odds than before, he acknowledged.

Not that it mattered. Whatever the odds, he was going to get Raine out of that house.

He managed to drag Elga down the first few steps, and then he closed the trap door over her, pushing the bolt home. When he picked up the shotgun again, he looked up at the mansion, silhouetted against the rain-shrouded darkness.

And this time he breathed the prayer he hadn't been hopeful enough to whisper before.

Chapter Twenty

When the knob of the back door moved under his hand, Ethan released the breath he'd not been aware he was holding. Elga Marguery must have left it unlocked when she'd come out into the rain. Not having to break into the house lessened the risk that he might be discovered before he was ready.

He eased the door open and then stepped into the dark hallway, pulling it closed behind him. There was a light coming from the room where Sabina had entertained them this afternoon. In the stillness he could hear voices, which also seemed to originate from there.

They were too low for him to identify, although the timbre of one was clearly masculine. And the other...

Despite listening for several seconds, he couldn't tell. Raine or the old woman?

He shifted the weight of the gun, supporting the heavy barrels with his left hand as the index finger on his right curled over one of the triggers. The double-barreled shotgun wouldn't have been his choice, but in this situation, having any sort of weapon was an unbelievable gift.

He began edging down the hallway, keeping his back to the wall opposite the room he was approaching. His shoes squelched slightly with each step. In spite of that noise, the tone of the conversation in the parlor never altered.

He hesitated before making the move that would bring him in line with the open doorway, allowing him to see into that room. He took a final look down the long hall toward the front door. There were no lights at all in that part of the house. It seemed everyone was gathered in the room across from him.

He took a deep breath, and then, in preparation for what he was about to do, he blew it out soundlessly through pursed lips. He lifted the shotgun and took the step that would position him before the door.

For a few seconds none of the three occupants of the room realized he was there. He had time to catalogue their positions, a procedure his training made automatic.

He had found Raine first. She was in a straight chair, her back to the door. He couldn't see her face, but the fact that she was sitting up was reassuring.

Directly in front of her was Charles Ellington. He was standing before the fireplace, one arm casually draped along the mantel. He held a whiskey glass in that hand, its amber liquid reflecting the lamplight.

The old woman was to Ethan's right, enthroned in the same chair from which she'd greeted them this afternoon. She spotted him first, dark eyes widening in shock before her mouth opened to shout a warning. He didn't understand the language in which the words were spoken, but their intent was clear.

Ellington's eyes lifted to the doorway. He straightened, as if preparing to move.

"Don't even think about it," Ethan warned, moving the deadly, side-by-side barrels so that they pointed at the psychologist's chest. "No matter how quick you are, some of this shot is bound to get you."

Ellington's chin lifted, and for a split second Ethan thought he was going to be foolish enough to put that to the test. His finger tightened over the trigger before the psychologist nodded his agreement, sagging back against the fireplace. Of course, Ellington had never struck Ethan as someone willing to fight—or to die—for his principles.

Hearing his voice, Raine had turned to face the doorway, revealing the black half mask over her eyes. With the handicap of the heavy weapon and his injuries, Ethan realized he couldn't remove it right now. Nor could he untie her.

That would have to wait until he had had the situation under control. In the meantime, for her own protection…

"Don't move, Raine. Not unless I tell you to."

Her mouth opened as if to protest that command, but she closed it quickly and nodded her understanding.

"Who's here besides Ellington?"

She shook her head, her forehead furrowing slightly, but she answered him. "Marguery."

Marguery. Raine had been right about the significance of that missing gravestone. Both Ellington and Sabina had lied.

The fact that Marguery had staged his own death a quarter of a century ago was a dead giveaway that he had recognized that his involvement in Cassandra not only spelled the end of his career, but, depending on what had been involved, maybe the end of his freedom. His supposed death had also provided him with the opportunity to pursue his personal agenda for the past twenty-five years without anyone being the wiser.

"And Sabina," Raine added unnecessarily.

The old woman was still shouting invectives at him as she struggled to get out of her chair. Ethan ignored her, deciding that any threat she might present would be negligible.

Marguery was the real danger. Ethan's gaze again swept the small parlor while he held Ellington pinned in place with the deadly barrels of the shotgun. Despite the shadowed corners where the light from the lamp didn't quite reach, it was obvious that there was no one else in the room.

"Where is he?"

"Marguery? He was right here."

Despite the blindfold, she turned her head as if trying to find him. Maybe her confusion was a result of concussion, Ethan thought. The bruise on her temple was livid.

"Think you can walk?" he asked.

He would carry her out of here if he had to, but it would be far easier if she could travel under her own steam.

"Of course."

There had been no hesitation in her answer, which made him feel marginally better. The only thing he had to worry about now was locating Marguery, the mastermind behind whatever had been going on. And possibly the connection he'd been seeking between Cassandra and The Covenant? Had the descendant of one of the founding families of this country decided he was better equipped to decide national policy than the elected officials?

That would make sense of Catherine Suttle's claim that the present-day organization was a continuation of one that had been around since the nation began. One James Marguery's ancestors had been a part of?

Some movement in his peripheral vision made him turn in time to see Sabina charging across the room. The cane that had rested by her chair this afternoon was now held in both hands and raised high in the air.

Ethan managed to get his arm up in time to protect his head. However, both that movement and the blow from the stick, although not particularly powerful, reverberated

along the broken collarbone. A wordless expression of ag
ony, like the noise a wounded animal might make, was tor
from his throat.

Despite his effort to steady the shotgun, the heavy barrel
drooped. Aware that he had given Ellington an opening, h
struggled to lift the weapon and bring it back into align
ment. His arm was numb, nerves and muscles uncoopera
tive.

"Get down," he shouted to Raine. Watching Ellington'
eyes, Ethan knew exactly when he reached his decision.

At the same time the old woman hit him again, strikin
him on the shoulder with the metal head of the cane. Eve
as he fought to control the unwieldy weight of the gun, h
swept his right foot out, catching Sabina at the ankles. Of
balance from her attack, she fell, grabbing his arm an
hanging on for a few vital seconds before he was finall
able to pull away, sending her sprawling to the floor.

The distraction had lasted long enough for Ellington t
make his move. The drawer to the table at the end of th
sofa gaped open. The revolver that had been hidden ther
was now in the psychologist's hand. He was sprinting to
ward Raine, careful to keep her between him and the muz
zle of the shotgun. Once he got to her, he would use he
as a shield to make his escape.

"Get down," Ethan shouted again.

Just as the psychologist reached her chair, Raine threw
herself onto the floor. Since she couldn't use her hands to
cushion her fall, she hit hard. Without a second's hesitation
she twisted her body, deliberately rolling it into the legs o
the man approaching from the fireplace.

Ellington sidestepped to avoid going down, but the
effort had been enough to disrupt his aim. The bullet from
the revolver splintered wood in the doorframe ove
Ethan's head.

The echo of that shot was lost in the roar of the shotgun. Ellington staggered backward. His hands, the right one still holding the weapon, attempted to cover the widespread pattern of buckshot that centered his chest.

He looked down, eyes widening as if surprised to find blood staining the pristine whiteness of his shirt and the open seersucker jacket. Then he lifted his head, mouth open, to meet Ethan's gaze. The look of surprise on his face hadn't faded.

The old woman was screaming again, a sound that echoed as loudly as the gunshot in the confines of the small room. Ellington spoke to her, the words gasped in the language she had used to her niece. Then he fell back against the fireplace, his free hand clutching the mantel.

Sabina reached him in time to help him slide bonelessly down the bricks until he was sitting on the hearth, legs stretched straight out before him. At first she tried to stanch the flow of blood using the white handkerchief from his breast pocket. Finally realizing it was hopeless, she began a high-pitched keening, obviously the sound of grief.

Ellington's hand reached out and blindly found the back of her head. He patted it as one might comfort a child before he pulled her against his shoulder, finally—mercifully—cutting off the noise. Ethan watched them, his finger on the trigger of the other barrel, until the hand that rested against that snow-white braid finally relaxed and then fell.

With the tableau the two of them presented, Ethan discovered the last piece of the puzzle. Raine had been right. Marguery *had* been in the room all along, only he'd been disguised as Charles Ellington.

There was no doubt in Ethan's mind that the man he'd just killed was the same one who had talked to them in Griff's office this morning, the respected British scientist who had supposedly worked on the CIA's parapsychology projects. Who had even written the definitive book on those. And if that *were* Marguery, then when and how had he taken on the persona of Ellington?

"Ethan?" Raine's voice.

"I'm here," he said. "Everything's okay. It's over."

He pulled his eyes away from the couple by the fireplace and closed the distance to Raine. He bent and pulled the blindfold over her head without bothering to untie the strings. She blinked against the sudden light, ducking until her eyes adjusted.

He took that opportunity to scan the room again, still wary of the unexpected. When his eyes returned to her face, she was looking up at him,

"Are you all right?" she asked.

It was the question he should have asked her. Unwilling to answer it, he broke the connection between them, looking again at the old woman, still sobbing against her husband's body.

"No wonder I didn't recognize him."

Raine sounded controlled. A little *too* controlled, considering what had just happened.

"*Was* there ever a Charles Ellington?"

"I didn't remember him this morning, but that isn't saying much. I didn't remember Sabina, either. Or my uncle. Not until tonight."

She had told him that Gardner had taken her away from her uncle. Now she seemed to be saying—

"*Marguery* was your uncle?"

"By marriage. Sabina was my aunt. My mother's sister. My flesh and blood," she added bitterly.

"Then…"

"No, Mr. Gardner *isn't* my father. I only wanted him to be. You can't imagine how much."

He wasn't sure what to say in the face of that admission,

not given the pain her claim had caused Gardner's family. That was something that would eventually have to resolved, but not tonight.

"Come on," he said, putting his left hand, the one that seemed to be functioning almost normally, under her elbow to help her up. "Let's get out of here."

"He murdered him." Raine was still looking up at him, but she had made no attempt to rise. "That's what I saw that night at the pond. My uncle slashed his wrists while he begged for his life, and then, when he was dead, together they dragged his body into the edge of the water and rolled it in."

Despite all he'd seen in his years with Cabot's team, a coldness settled in his stomach at the description of that brutality. And he wasn't a five-year-old girl.

"Ellington? You're saying your uncle killed Ellington."

She nodded. "I didn't know why they were doing it, but I understood enough…" The words trailed.

She had been a child, and she had witnessed the kind of unspeakable violence she had chosen to step away from as an adult. The fact that it had touched her so personally and at such a vulnerable age made her decision far more understandable.

"I'd forgotten all of it until today," she said.

"The pond brought it back?"

"Sabina, first, I think. I knew I'd heard the phrasing she used before. The language you couldn't identify. The smell of her cigarettes, the same as my mother smoked. It was all tantalizingly familiar, but I couldn't remember. For so long I hadn't *wanted* to remember, and then when I did…"

"Come on," he said when she ran down.

This time she let him help her up. When she was standing beside him, he laid down the shotgun in preparation of removing her bonds. Before he did, he had to physically restrain himself from taking her into his arms. *Later. After this is finished. There'll be plenty of time....*

It was the same argument he'd made last night, he realized. And then today, time had almost run out. For both of them.

He gathered her to him with his good arm, hugging her tightly despite the fact that her hands were still tied. After a moment he held her away from him, looking down into her face to make sure she really was all right. What he saw reassured him enough to turn her so that her back was to him.

"And I know why Mr. Gardner destroyed Cassandra," she said as he began to unfasten her bonds.

"You're saying that *Monty* closed down the project?"

She nodded, rubbing her newly freed wrists to restore the circulation. "He discovered that Cassandra wasn't designed to spy on the Russians. My uncle was spying on Americans. On anyone he suspected of having allegiances to other ideologies."

Ethan wondered why Gardner hadn't mentioned any of this when he'd sent them to Raine. Maybe because he, like everyone else, had really believed Marguery was dead. And because he had never seen any link between Cassandra and The Covenant.

As soon as Marguery found out they'd visited the former DCI, however, he believed the Phoenix had made that crucial connection. He'd tried and failed to get rid of the old man.

When Ethan had taken Raine back to Washington, it had thrown them into panic mode. First the attack at the hospital, with the unknown member of The Covenant posing as an agent. Then the attempt on the night of the fundraiser. There was no doubt that if Raine hadn't fled onto that ledge that night, Marguery would have killed her. She knew far too much. Or so he thought.

"And he was using you to do the spying?"

"I can't imagine that the method could be very efficient—"

"What is it?" Ethan asked when she stopped.

Slowly she raised her eyes to his. They were wide and dark in the shadowed room.

"Or maybe it was."

"What do you mean?"

"I don't think Ellington was the first."

Not the first person Marguery had killed? If her uncle were involved in The Convenant, with their plots to fund domestic terror, then it shouldn't surprise him that he was guilty of multiple murders. Raine, however, was clearly devastated by the memories tonight's events had unlocked. As she'd said, these people were her flesh and blood.

"Let it go," he said, putting his hand under her elbow.

"What if when I gave him the information—"

"Stop it." His voice harsh. "You were a kid. You had no idea what he was doing. You couldn't have. Besides, you aren't sure…" He hesitated, unwilling to complete that thought.

"Sometimes I overheard them. They thought I was too young to understand what they were saying, but I understood the words. I didn't always understand what they *meant,* but now…"

"You have to let it go, Raine. If you don't—"

"It will drive me insane?" she asked with a small, bitter laugh. "It's a little late for that, don't you think?"

"You're the sanest person I know."

"Given your background, that isn't saying much."

Despite her taunt, he pulled her to him again, wrapping his good arm around her. She leaned against him willingly, as if she knew this was where she belonged. Next to his heart.

"It's over. Marguery's dead. He can't hurt anyone anymore. Especially not you. Not if you refuse to let him."

She nodded, her head moving against his chest. Her fingers had tightened around the material of his shirt, holding on to him. It was an emotion he certainly understood. When he had walked past that cruiser...

"What do we do now?"

Good question. He again considered Sabina Marguery, who was still stroking her dead husband's head. No longer a threat, but someone who would have to be dealt with. And he wasn't going to call the locals to do it.

"We call Cabot," he said. "Tying up the loose ends, especially if they're politically sensitive—as I suspect a lot of this will be—is Griff's specialty. We're going to hand this one over to him."

Chapter Twenty-One

"You were a child," Monty Gardner said. "How could any of it have been your fault?"

During the seemingly endless week since James Marguery's death, Raine had spent most of her time talking to representatives of one national security agency or another. The news that, on the same day she and Ethan had driven to Mrytlewood, Mr. Gardner had regained consciousness and seemed to have no damage was almost all that had kept her going.

This afternoon was the first time the old man had been allowed visitors other than family. Although Griff had offered to arrange for her to see him, Raine had insisted on following the rules. She'd done enough damage with her fantasy.

"I could have told you what I saw that night." Raine was sitting on the edge of his bed, holding both Gardner's hands in hers.

"You probably couldn't have," Cabot said. "Not him. Not anyone."

"I don't understand."

"What you saw, combined with what you'd suffered at the hands of your uncle, would almost certainly have kept you quiet. And as soon as Monty removed you from his influence, your mind set about creating an alternate reality to the one you had been living.''

An alternate reality. Almost her entire life could be reduced to that phrase.

So much of what she had believed were things she had fabricated to replace the events her mind couldn't deal with, until ultimately the reality had been wiped from her memory. And that made her feel more like a freak than her gift ever had.

"*Forgetting* was exactly what I had hoped you'd do,'' Gardner said. "At the time I had no idea how much you needed to forget.''

"And you never had any inkling that Marguery had faked his own death?'' Cabot asked.

"You're thinking I should have,'' the former DCI accused, "but I had no reason to doubt his suicide. I fired Marguery as soon as I found out what he was doing with Project Cassandra. No one was sorry to see him go. He was already persona non grata with most of the agency because of his arrogance. And his wife, of course.''

"Because they thought she was Russian?'' Raine asked.

"Because she wasn't as adept at hiding her prejudices as Jimmy was.''

"What kind of prejudices?'' Ethan asked.

Raine was physically aware of him, of course, every time they were in the same room, which hadn't been very often since those events at Myrtlewood.

They had both been busy dealing with the fallout, part of which had been that a female FBI agent had replaced Ethan as her bodyguard. Raine had tried to convince herself that the reason for that was nothing more than a medical issue. Ethan was still wearing his right arm in a sling, and she knew from the careful way he moved that his ribs were still painful.

"Sabina was an equal-opportunity hater," Gardner said in answer to Ethan's question. "The Russians. Jews. Muslims. And she made no bones about any of it. Although we hadn't reached the heights of political correctness Washington has since attained, her rabidity didn't go over particularly well in the rather select community her husband belonged to."

"Since her country had fallen under Soviet dominance," Ethan said, "I can understand her hatred of the Russians, but the others…?"

"Anti-Semitism has always had deep roots in Eastern Europe. The hatred of the Muslims went back to their conquest of her country centuries ago. That was especially true within her culture."

"Her culture?" Raine asked.

"You didn't know? No, how could you?" the old man said. "Sabina was Romany."

Romany. Rom. Gypsies. The outcasts of Europe. It took only a second for Raine to make that progression in her mind. And less than that to make the next.

"Did she have the gift?"

"If she had, she wouldn't have needed you."

"*Sabina?*" Cabot questioned the old man's wording. "Why did Sabina need Raine?"

"To get the one thing she wanted more than anything else in the world."

"Marguery," Raine said softly.

"The difference in their ages was obvious. She must have been fifteen years older. What *wasn't* obvious was why someone as brilliant as Jimmy Marguery would tie himself to a woman who was despised by everyone he knew."

"She had brought him Raine?" Griff suggested.

"When the agency tapped Jimmy to head up our answer

to the Russian's experiments in parapsychology, he began to discreetly put out feelers for psychics. Some of those feelers were undoubtedly made to the Romany population in the States, who quickly passed them on to the European communities.

"I don't remember the details," Gardner went on, "but eventually someone set up a meeting with Sabina. I *do* remember that he was reluctant to make the trip behind the Iron Curtain. Ironically, he didn't like operating undercover. When he met you with your aunt and found out how talented you were, he was willing to do anything to bring you back here."

"Including marrying Sabina," Ethan guessed.

The old man nodded. "I don't know how she made him stick to his bargain for so long, but she did. At least his 'suicide' freed him from her constant company."

Despite her feelings about her aunt, the image of the old woman's grief was still fresh. Whatever her aunt's faults, she had loved James Marguery. Judging by his final action, he may even have grown to appreciate her devotion.

"From what I've heard about him," Cabot said, "suicide would seem out of character."

"I'd destroyed his life's work as well as his reputation, at least within the agency. At the time of his death, he hadn't worked in several years. I don't think anyone at the CIA thought to question that he had taken his own life. We certainly had no reason to suspect he'd taken someone else's instead. And remember, we weren't as sophisticated in those days. There was no DNA testing."

"He probably chose Ellington because physically they were the same type," Griff said. "And perhaps because the man was a British national. There was no family here to report him missing."

"As I recall, it took a while before they discovered the

body. Being in the water all that time…'' Gardner shrugged. ''Identification would probably have been made by Marguery's wife.''

''And the local sheriff was in Marguery's pocket.'' Ethan's injuries were a constant reminder of exactly how deep in his pocket that department had been.

''The agency might have checked dental records,'' Gardner said, ''but for someone with as much experience in intel as Jimmy had, it would have been easy enough arrange an exchange of his and Ellington's.''

''So Ellington *did* work for the CIA?''

''Not on those projects. Not that I remember. As a psychologist, I suppose he could have done some contract work, but…'' The old man shook his head.

''Ellington's book was based on Marguery's work,'' Cabot said. ''Who better to write it than the man himself?''

''That was the kind of arrogance at which Jimmy excelled. He obviously believed he was far too clever to be caught. Certainly not after twenty-five years.''

''That arrogance might also explain why he kept the records of The Covenant in a safe at Myrtlewood,'' Cabot said. ''The FBI is having a field day with those.''

''Then he *was* involved,'' Gardner said.

''He fancied himself as carrying on his family's noble tradition of protecting this country. Much of the material is couched in those terms.''

''There are references in what the Bureau found to the Illuminati, an organization many of the founding fathers were rumored to belong to,'' Ethan added.

''Crazy bastard,'' the old man said. And then, glancing back at Raine, ''Forgive me, my dear, but it's such a tragedy to see a good mind so twisted.''

''Judging by Cassandra, it always was,'' she said.

Acting on the information she'd provided them, the FBI

had drained the pond at Myrtlewood and were in the process of identifying the bones that had been found in its deepest part. Even though Marguery had been working for the agency at that time, she didn't see any reason to tell Mr. Gardner about those murders. Not yet. He would learn that particular detail about Cassandra soon enough.

"I think that's enough talk for one day," Griff said, seeming to realize, as she had, that they were treading dangerously near information Gardner didn't need to hear. Not at this fragile stage of his recovery. "Later on I'm sure the Bureau will want to hear what you know about Marguery."

The old man's eyes had brightened at the suggestion, but he didn't protest their intent to leave. His face looked pinched and drawn, the bruises still colorful.

He reached out and patted Raine's hand. "Don't let them keep you too busy to visit. There's no reason not to now."

Any danger Marguery or Sabina might have represented to her was finally over. If her uncle had only known that she'd blocked the memories of her former life, it would have been over long ago. Of course, if he had known that, he wouldn't have made the fatal error in judgment that had led to his downfall.

"I have one more question before I go," she said.

Griff shrugged slightly, which she took as permission. She turned back to Monty Gardner, whom she knew now had probably saved not only her life but also her sanity.

"Do you know anything about my mother and father?"

The small hope she'd nurtured since her memory had returned died when he shook his head.

"After I shut down Cassandra, I tried to find them, but Sabina, or Jimmy, acting on her behalf, had covered the trail too well. There was no way to trace your family."

"Thank you for trying," she said, burying her disappointment by leaning forward to press a kiss against his cheek. "Thank you for everything."

"If I had only known sooner—"

"I know," she said, straightening to smile at him. "And now we really do need to leave you to get some rest."

"Come back soon," he urged as she stood and began to walk to the door of the hospital room.

"As soon as I can. You and I have some catching up to do."

She stepped out into the hall to give Cabot and Ethan the opportunity to say goodbye. The door swung shut behind her only to open immediately as Cabot emerged from the room. In his hand was the small black jeweler's box she had sent back to him two days ago.

He held it out to her with a smile. "A peace offering."

"I can't take these."

"He wants you to have them. You can ask him if you don't believe me. Just not now."

"I thought you said he'd already given me too much."

"I was wrong. About a lot of things. As I said, consider these a peace offering. Or an apology, if you prefer."

She shook her head. "Give them to Claire. She has far more right to them."

"Claire's had her full share of both his love and his generosity. They really were his grandmother's, you know. I'm not sure how you knew that, but you were right."

She smiled, acknowledging the concession he'd just made. "It's no different than using something that belongs to a missing child. The connection is still there, somehow embodied in an object they cherished."

"Then cherish these. As she must have." Griff took her hand and, putting the box into it, wrapped her fingers around the edge. "After all, he has already given you her name."

She didn't protest again. "Will you tell Claire how sorry I am?"

"She got your note. I think she understands. As much as she can. It's hard for most people to imagine…"

"I know," Raine said when he hesitated. "Sometimes it's hard for me, too."

The door to the hospital room opened again, and Ethan stepped out into the hall. His eyes met Cabot's. With whatever unspoken communication passed between them, the Phoenix head quickly made his excuses, leaving them in the hallway alone.

"How are you?" Raine asked finally after the silence grew almost unbearable.

His injuries were the only safe subject she could think of. Everything else seemed fraught with too many emotional pitfalls.

"You didn't return my calls," he said.

"I know. I'm sorry. I meant to, but… There are so many questions I don't have answers for."

"About me?"

Smiling, she shook her head. "I told you. There are *some* advantages to what I do." The only important questions she'd ever had about Ethan Snow had been answered almost as soon as she met him.

"Then…you didn't call because you didn't want to see me."

He looked tired. And he sounded hurt. She had never intended that, but she should have known he would be.

"You must know better than that."

He looked away, his eyes focusing somewhere over her head. When they came back to her face, she ached for what was in them.

"I've never felt about another woman in my life the way

I feel about you. I thought…'' He hesitated and then closed his mouth, his lips flat.

''You weren't wrong.''

''Then what the hell is going on? Why are you so damned distant?''

''Because everything I believed about my life is a lie. Something my mind created because it didn't like the reality.''

Griff had insisted she see a psychiatrist to help her understand exactly what had happened to her. The thing that had frightened her most was the dissociative episode she'd suffered the night of the fund-raising dinner.

Had she been so frightened by the sound of Marguery's voice that she had tried to escape by climbing out on the ledge? And then remembered nothing about it? If her mind could play that kind of trick, who could say for sure that the same thing might not happen in the future?

Until she knew it wouldn't, she couldn't make the kind of commitment she had dreamed of only days ago. It wouldn't be fair to Ethan. It wouldn't be fair to either of them.

''It was a way of dealing with what you'd experienced,'' he said. ''Thousands of people have done—''

''I'm not thousands of people. I'm just…me. Someone who climbed out on a ledge to escape who she really is.''

''You climbed out on a ledge to escape someone who had brutalized you. Someone you'd seen commit a particularly gruesome murder. I wouldn't say that was…''

''Insane?'' she finished when he hesitated.

''Is that what you're afraid of?''

He had cut to the heart of her fear, but it was one she didn't intend to articulate again. Even admitting to worrying about that gave it credence, at least in her mind.

"I need some time to sort it all out," she said instead. "To understand what happened. And to accept it."

"How much time?"

"I don't know."

"Damn it, Raine."

"That isn't even my name. It's the name Gardner gave me. I'd forgotten my own *name*, Ethan."

"It doesn't matter."

"It does to me. And because of that, if for no other reason, it should matter to you."

"That isn't fair."

"I know. None of it is. But I'm asking you to do it, anyway. Just give me a little time."

His eyes fell. When he raised them again, she knew that she had won.

"I'm holding you to that. 'A little time.'"

She nodded. And then, because she couldn't resist, she stepped forward, laying her cheek against his chest. The scent of his body was almost enough to make her break the agreement she had just insisted they make.

His left arm came around her, holding her close. He put his chin against the top of her head and then pressed his lips there.

She closed her eyes, savoring the feel of being in his arms again. She couldn't remember a time when she had ever felt this safe. He had protected her through everything that had happened these last two weeks. She knew he always would.

That would have been enough for most women. It should have been enough for her. The problem was that she wanted to come to him whole. An equal partner rather than someone he would again have to take care of.

She had had her fill of that, as grateful as she was to Monty Gardner for what he'd done. It was time for her to find out who Raine McAllister was and what she was capable of. And until she had...

She stepped back, moving out of Ethan's embrace. It was the most difficult thing she had ever had to do in her life.

His face was set, unrevealing, but she knew he was fighting the same emotions she was. She put her hand against his cheek, feeling the muscle clench and unclench beneath the masculine roughness of his skin.

"I love you," she whispered, and then, before she could change her mind, she turned and walked down that long hospital corridor alone.

Epilogue

Three Months Later

Her late-night walk along the shore had become almost a ritual. It not only helped to fill the long, empty hours until she could go to bed, but the physical activity helped her sleep.

If she concentrated on the beauty of the moonlight on top of the water or on the sound of the waves, there were even stretches of time during which she managed not to think of Ethan at all. Precious minutes during which she could also lock those long-suppressed memories out of her head once more.

Tonight's expedition had been more successful than most. The peace she had always found in this setting seemed to again be healing her spirit. Now if she could only be sure she was doing the right thing as far as Ethan was concerned....

She glanced up, trying to locate the light she'd left on the back deck of her house and realized she was much closer to home than she'd thought. She had somehow lost track of both time and place. And she was infinitely grateful there was nothing to fear about that. Not any longer.

Before she stepped out of the edge of the surf to head

across the sand, her eyes focused farther down the beach. The moonlight revealed a man standing almost directly behind her house, the incoming tide foaming whitely around his feet.

There was an indefinable something about the set of his head and the lean strength of his body that was instantly recognizable. Not only had she shaped those long bones and hard muscles while sculpting the figure of the runner, she had explored every powerful inch of them with her lips and tongue. She would have known Ethan Snow in her sleep.

She *had* known him. In countless erotic dreams since her return from Washington.

As she watched him, the waves continued to roll inexorably to shore between them. There was no other sound. No other motion.

Mentally she called to him, consciously electing to use the gift she had once rejected. If she had learned nothing else in the time she had spent in Washington, she had learned that. Her abilities were an integral part of who and what she was, and they always would be. Anyone who loved her...

Ethan turned his head, looking down the beach to where she stood unaware until now that her forward progress had stopped. She held her breath, waiting for whatever came next.

After a moment he began walking toward her. After a step or two, he began to run, long legs eating the distance between them, the motion as smooth and athletic as that portrayed by the runner she'd fashioned before she met him.

As he drew nearer, his stride slowed until he was once more walking. He had discarded his shoes, and although the cuffs of the khaki trousers he wore had been turned up a few times, their material was stained with saltwater. His white dress shirt was unbuttoned at the throat.

She noted those unimportant details before she dared to look at his face. The gray eyes were silvered by the moonlight, his lips unsmiling, their expression almost stern.

He came to a halt perhaps ten feet away from her, searching her face. "Raine?"

"I didn't know you were coming."

There was a small silence.

"Neither did I."

As difficult as that was to hear, she knew it was the truth. This was something he had resisted because she had asked him to.

"But I'm glad you're here," she confessed.

"I wasn't sure," he said. "You seemed…"

"Distracted by the moonlight," she said when he hesitated, and then she smiled at him.

He glanced out at the ocean where the rising moon cast its silver arrow across the water. The depth of the breath he took lifted his shoulders before he turned back to look at her.

"I don't understand. What does that mean?"

Nothing. Everything.

"Why are you here?" she asked, ignoring his question.

"Because I couldn't wait any longer."

"Is that an ultimatum?"

"It's a confession."

One very few men would have made. And the fact that he had…

"I needed to see you," he said. "I needed to know you're all right."

"I'm fine," she said, smiling at him. "No more ledges. No more dissociative episodes."

"I didn't mean that."

"I know, but...maybe I needed to tell you. I've been seeing someone to help me come to grips with what happened. You were right, you know."

"About what?"

"How common this is. How...normal, for want of a better word. Especially in children. It's a form of self-protection."

"And now that you know that?"

"It's not nearly so terrifying."

"Good."

"It also probably explains why I couldn't cope with the other."

"With the abducted children?"

"What was happening to them in some way brought back what had happened to me. I didn't want those memories to resurface, so I chose to avoid contact with the evil that threatened them."

"Self-protection," he reminded softly.

"Or cowardice."

"No."

She hadn't realized how much she needed to hear him say that. Not until he had.

She would deal with her own guilt, but it helped to know that the bravest person she'd ever met didn't judge her. Just like the cops she'd worked with so long.

"I've also learned that I can't change what I am," she said. "And I can't stop using what I've been given."

"I know."

"And, Ethan... Neither can you."

The silence stretched a long time, broken only by the sound of the waves at their feet.

"I know," he said, repeating the affirmation she had made.

Whether for the Phoenix or for someone else, Ethan

would use the gifts *he* had been given. To fight injustice. To protect those who were unable to protect themselves. They were as much a part of who and what he was as her gift was a part of her. They were not to be squandered. Or denied.

"I spoke to Mr. Gardner before I left Washington."

"How is he?"

"He wants you to come and live with him. I promised I'd give you the message."

"I can't do that, but…it means a great deal that he would ask me."

"His isn't the only offer you have."

"It's the only one I've heard so far."

"Maybe you're too far away."

Smiling, she took the few steps that separated them. She stopped, looking up into his eyes.

They were far more beautiful than she had remembered. He was more beautiful than the figure her clumsy efforts in the studio had created. So beautiful her heart ached with the unaccustomed joy of having him here.

"Close enough?"

"Not quite."

He bent, closing the distance between them. Although she had been expecting his kiss, he pressed his lips against her forehead before he leaned back, looking down into her eyes.

"I've missed you," he said.

"I know."

"Do you know everything?"

"Enough. I know that you're here."

"Does that mean you're going to let me stay?"

"Tonight at least."

The smile in his eyes faded. "And then?"

"Then you have work to do. And so do I."

"What kind of work?"

"It's okay," she said, responding to the concern she heard in his careful question. "There's no reason for me not to do it now. And a lot of very good ones for me to go back."

"Helping the cops with their missing children." His voice was flat.

"Please don't worry. I'm not nearly so fragile as you seem to think."

"What I think is that for you to have survived, intact and functioning, means you're tough enough to give a couple of the old hands at the Phoenix a run for their money."

She laughed. "Will you tell me which ones they are when I meet them?"

When I meet them...

He was thinking about the phrasing. Trying to find any other interpretation for it before he believed her. And when he couldn't...

"You're coming back with me." It was not a question.

"Unless you think Mr. Cabot is going to open a branch of the Phoenix down here."

"I have to warn you," he said, "my family is fairly conservative."

"Meaning I can't put up a sign outside advertising Tarot readings?"

"Meaning they would be far more welcoming of Mr. and Mrs. Ethan Snow."

She hadn't expected that. Not yet, at least.

"Is that a proposal?"

"Didn't it sound like one? I can try again."

"Then I'd like the 'Will you marry me?' version, if you don't mind."

"Will you, Raine McAllister, take this man to be your lawfully wedded husband?"

"Lorraine," she corrected before she stood on tiptoe to meet his lips. "You always use full names during the ceremony."

"I wasn't sure you were keeping it."

"Why wouldn't I? My first name was bestowed on me by someone I love very much. And my last name…"

"Your last name," he prompted as he finally broke the long, deep kiss that had interrupted whatever she'd been about to say.

"Will be bestowed on me by someone whom I love even better. And will love even longer. Far longer," she whispered, the last word lost as his lips covered hers again.

Until death do us part…

Ethan would love her forever, just as the vows they would take promised. She knew that with as much certainty as she had ever known anything in her life.

There were, after all, *some* advantages to what she did.

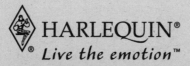

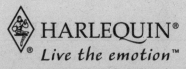

"Sexy, funny and a little outrageous,
Leslie Kelly is a must read!"
—*New York Times* bestselling author Carly Phillips

National bestselling author

LESLIE KELLY

Killing Time

She's got TV ratings—and legs—to die for!

When a reality TV show rolls
into his small hometown,
Mick Winchester is reunited
with Caroline Lamb, his
college sweetheart and one
true love. But suddenly a
real corpse turns up on
the set and things become
all too real....

*A riveting read you
won't want to miss...
coming in August 2004!*

HARLEQUIN®
Live the emotion™

www.eHarlequin.com

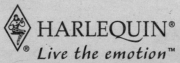

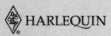

HARLEQUIN

INTRIGUE

COMING NEXT MONTH

#789 BULLETPROOF BILLIONAIRE by Mallory Kane
New Orleans Confidential

New Orleans Confidential agent Seth Lewis took on the alias of a suave international tycoon to infiltrate the Cajun Mob. He'd set out to gain entry by charming the rich widow Adrienne DeBlanc into telling him everything. It wasn't long before his protective instincts surfaced for the fragile beauty, but could he risk a high-stakes case for love?

#790 MIDNIGHT DISCLOSURES by Rita Herron
Nighthawk Island

In one tragic moment, radio psychologist Dr. Claire Kos had lost everything. She survived, only to become a serial killer's next target. Blind and vulnerable to attack, she turned to FBI agent Mark Steele—the man she'd loved and lost. As the killer took aim, Mark was poised to protect the woman he couldn't live without.

#791 ON THE LIST by Patricia Rosemoor
Club Undercover

Someone wanted to silence agent Renata Fox for good. She knew the Feds had accused the wrong person of being the Chicago sniper, but her speculations had somehow landed her on the real killer's hit list. So when Gabriel Connor showed up claiming he was on the assassin's trail, Renata knew she had to put her life—and her heart—in Gabe's hands....

#792 A DANGEROUS INHERITANCE by Leona Karr
Eclipse

When a storm delivered heiress Stacy Ashford into the iron-hard embrace of Josh Spencer, it seemed their meeting was fated. Gaining her inheritance depended on reopening the eerie hotel where Josh's kid sister died. And even though Stacy's inheritance bound them to an ever-tightening coil of danger, would Josh's oath to avenge his sister cost him the one woman who truly mattered?

#793 INTENSIVE CARE by Jessica Andersen

When Dr. Ripley Davis saw another of her patients flatline, she knew someone was killing the people in her care. But before she could find the real murderer, overbearing, impossibly sexy police officer Zachary Cage accused her of the crime. It wasn't long before her fiery resolve convinced him she wasn't the prime suspect...she was the prime *target*.

#794 SUDDEN ALLIANCE by Jackie Manning

When undercover operative Liam O'Shea found Sarah Regis on the side of the road, battered and incoherent, his razor-sharp instincts warned him she was in danger. As an amnesic murder witness, her only hope for survival was to stay in close proximity to Liam. Would their sudden alliance survive the secrets she'd kept locked inside?

www.eHarlequin.com